SYNNR'S RIDE

FATED MATE ALIEN ROMANCE

ZULIR WARRIOR MATES
BOOK FIVE

KATE RUDOLPH

ABOUT THE BOOK

Sparks fly when an alien soldier and an enemy spy must work together to win a war...

Jori Harek is a loyal Synnr soldier.

He's determined to get to the bottom of Apsyn treachery and root out the rot before the enemies make any more headway onto his home moon. It's a job he's proud to do, but when he's asked to infiltrate a gang of Apsyn sympathizers, his limits are tested.

Hanna Karsyn is a reformed Apsyn spy.

When Hanna finds out just how far her superiors were willing to go to win the war, she walked straight into the arms of the Synnr military... and straight into a holding cell. Her only chance at freedom lies in helping Jori infiltrate a gang and uncover a cell of saboteurs.

Though there's no time for romance, each moment Jori and Hanna spend together creates an unquenchable blaze between them - one neither can deny, even as their passion puts both of their futures at risk.

1

THE GUARD WALKED by her cell three minutes past the hour. Hanna listened for the footsteps and counted it off.

Thirty seconds from her door to the bend in the hall. Forty steps at a sedate pace. This one walked a little faster. Thirty-six steps until his echo disappeared.

Hanna had six minutes.

She sat up.

Her wrists were bruised from the restraints they'd decided to use in the last interrogation. It didn't matter that she'd promised to cooperate, that going back home meant certain death. To these Synnrs, she was worse than a traitor.

She was a spy.

Or she used to be.

And that gave her a specific set of skills.

She had a piece of wire she'd managed to secret away. Whether it was the gods smiling up at her or something else, Hanna didn't know. But the lock on her door was simple. No need to hack electronics. A pick would do the trick.

The interrogation room was in the same direction the guard had walked, and so were the kitchens. Her second night in custody she'd been taken there and given a meal of Synnr delicacies she'd have paid a fortune for back on Kilrym.

She'd thought it was a preview of things to come. Fine food, nice treatment. All so long as she upheld her end of the deal and gave the Synnrs all the information she had.

Unfortunately, they didn't believe her when she told them she didn't know much.

She'd been living on military rations for weeks. Sure, they kept her fed, but the packs of dehydrated food were worse than flavorless. They were little piles of mush that somehow tasted like sweaty socks and dust.

She was pretty sure they were expired, too.

Five minutes.

She was guessing at this point. In the last three

weeks, her life had narrowed down to two hallways and a clock set by the guard rotation.

And Jori.

But she wasn't thinking about *him* right now.

She was almost certain she knew where she was. Right in the heart of Osais, the Synnr capitol of their home moon Aorsa. The Synnrs had rebelled and taken control of the moon centuries ago and sparked the fighting that had plagued almost every generation since. Their military had a training and administration building not far from the palace, the home of the false queen.

Hanna had to be there. It was where she'd been taken the day she'd surrendered herself to Synnr custody, and unless they'd been very clever, she hadn't been moved.

But she had to sleep sometime. And if the Synnrs had drugged her to move her, she could be anywhere.

No. She saw the same interrogators every couple of days. She saw *Jori* nearly every day. The Synnrs wouldn't inconvenience themselves. She was in the city.

Four minutes.

There should be another guard. This place wasn't a high security prison, but she was still a high value detainee. You didn't put only one guard on duty, not unless you were trying to save money and willing to risk your entire operation.

So, yes, a guard at the next door.

Hanna's fingers curled into fists. She could take out one guard. Maybe two. Her spark was electric in her veins. She hadn't accessed her power in days except to let her wings out every so often. It made some of her interrogators uncomfortable. Synnrs were more circumspect with their wings, keeping them contained unless they were using them.

Hanna's wings were gorgeous, swirling greens and golds with a hint of black the priest at her old temple said was a gift from Braznon himself.

But she couldn't put them on display if she was escaping from a military facility.

Luckily, she didn't need them to use her spark.

She could handle one guard. But two? Hanna wasn't a soldier, she was a spy. Well, more of a contractor with spy adjacent abilities. If she was doing her job right, she never had to fight anyone.

Three minutes. She was running out of time and still in the corridor.

Taking the guard's clothes was her best option. She could blend in with the other Synnr soldiers, slip out, and be on her way.

And where would she go?

Hanna stopped her internal clock and slumped back against her bed. The springs creaked, and the whole thing felt like it might collapse if she sat down too quickly or turned over in her sleep with too much force.

She couldn't escape.

Or, rather, she *could* escape, but that would screw her over even more.

That final question haunted her. Where would she go? Where *could* she go? She'd burned every bridge with one flash of her spark on her last mission. She couldn't bring herself to regret it. If she hadn't...

War brought out the worst in people, but she hadn't thought the Apsyn high command would sink so low.

What did that make her? She'd betrayed her Apsyn supervisors, ensured they wouldn't receive a piece of tech that could have led to a turning point in this useless war, and handed herself over to Synnr mercy. Was she still Apsyn? Was she a Synnr now? Was there some category in between for Zulir who weren't sure what side of the divide they fell on?

It wasn't just that Hanna had no place to go. She was a resourceful person and in the biggest city on this moon. If she needed, she could forge a new path for herself. She could leave her old name, her old identity behind and become a whole new woman.

But the escape would have to be flawless. If she got caught breaking out, that would evaporate whatever goodwill she'd earned from the Synnrs and she'd likely be thrown in a true prison.

And she'd prove Jori right.

Hanna curled up even tighter on the bed and ignored the creak of the springs. She shouldn't be giving Jorissan Harek a single thought. He was just another spy-breaker, a Synnr who looked at her so intensely his spark lit up his eyes.

And hers reacted.

No one else had that effect on her. No one else would sit across from her in the interrogation room and stare at her silently for an hour before walking away without saying a word. If she really had information on Apsyn secrets, he would have gotten them from her.

She didn't know how to convince him that he already had everything she knew.

Really, focusing on him was foolish. He was a Synnr, just like all the others. It didn't matter that looking at him, taking in all that intensity sent a thrill down her spine and awakened an awareness in other parts of her body that really shouldn't have been paying attention.

She really was a terrible spy. If she'd been any good at it, Hanna would have taken these feelings and used them against him. In that other life, she could have turned on the charm and seduced him.

That startled a laugh out of her.

She'd never seen the man smile. He was all seriousness and intensity when he sat down in that chair. And he was determined to pry her apart, one piece at a time. He wasn't thinking about seduction. And neither should she.

Hanna wasn't hiding anything from these Synnrs, but it didn't mean she could let her guard down. And she couldn't let Jorissan Harek get under her skin.

She wouldn't let him be her weakness.

———

Lips trailed down Jori's chest, slim fingers sliding along his side until he shivered. He arched into the touch, savoring the contact and letting it light him up. Flecks of his partner's spark danced over his skin, threatening to consume him.

It was dangerous play. Misjudge the power and he could end up fried.

But he liked to live dangerously.

He groaned as fingers wrapped around his cock, stroking firmly just the way he liked. And when her lips joined her fingers, he was lost. Jori surrendered himself to sensation, weaving his fingers through her soft hair and taking all that she would give him.

He wanted it all.

And if he wasn't completely overcome with the pleasure of it, he would have pulled her up, captured her lips with his own, and driven himself deep inside of her until they were so totally bound there was no disentangling them.

It was pleasure and torture combined. And there was more of their spark, even stronger now. It hovered over his skin and arced around him, more dangerous than before. But it felt too good to worry, this wasn't a battle, and if their play was too intense, it would only add to the pleasure.

She pulled off his cock and he tried to chase her, desperate and uncaring how it made him look. This was pleasure for both of them, and she deserved to know how she made him feel.

Anticipation made his spark even stronger. Strands of her dark hair rose up of their own accord, the electricity setting it off.

He was on the edge now, and it wouldn't take more than a breath to go tumbling over.

"Jori," she breathed out on a sigh, and looked up to meet his eyes.

Hanna.

Jori's spark flashed with one more violent bright light as he was pulled out of the dream. The nightmare.

The fantasy.

His cock was hard and aching, and it wouldn't take more than a few tugs to send him flying. Instead he curled his fingers against the edge of his bed and tried to will it away.

He wasn't some green recruit who lost it over a pretty face and wicked smile. Hanna Karsyn was an Apsyn spy, a woman in custody of the Synnr military, who'd nearly killed one of his comrades along with an innocent young woman who'd gotten mixed up in her plotting.

She wasn't someone he could afford to fantasize about.

There were millions of women in Osais.

Why was his cock so focused on this one?

His cock jerked and he groaned, a mix of pleasure and frustration.

Before Hanna Karsyn had crossed his path a

month earlier, things had been simple. He found a woman, he smiled, he flirted. They went out a time or two and had their fun, and then they both walked away satisfied.

He could always find someone else.

He hadn't bothered to look since the first day he saw Hanna.

Every time they met, it was a new challenge. He'd seen her spark dancing in her eyes and knew his own spark had done the same. One day this insane obsession had driven him so hard that he'd pulled her into an interrogation room and simply looked at her for the better part of an hour.

He'd told himself then he was trying to unnerve her.

Jori didn't like to lie. But he was getting very good at lying to himself.

If he had her alone... if the place wasn't wired for observation... if he asked and she said yes.

Jori wrapped his fingers around his cock and pumped, gritting his teeth against the pleasure as if this was some kind of punishment, some kind of ritual he was inflicting on himself to prove... something.

He groaned as he came, the image of Hanna fresh in his mind.

Of course she was in his mind. She was his days and his nights. Now she even ruled his dreams.

If he wasn't careful, she would have him wrapped around her fingers.

And she wasn't even trying.

In his apartment, the sanctuary away from the blood and death and order of the military, Jori could admit the truth, if only to himself.

Hanna Karsyn wasn't trying to play him. This undeniable attraction, this force that had wrapped itself around his cock and burrowed deep into his nervous system, was something much simpler. And more sinister.

He was attracted. And because he couldn't have her, he couldn't stop thinking about her.

Jori didn't normally have to face rejection.

If he smiled at a woman, if he flirted, she usually flirted back. He found women everywhere. Bars, the shop where he dropped off his laundry, the library.

But never at work.

The Synnr military was Jori's life. If it wasn't for his rank, he'd still be some kid bouncing around from orphanage to orphanage hoping one day for a family to pick him.

As if there weren't thousands of other war orphans they could choose.

He had to end this, somehow. Dedication to the work was one thing, but obsession had no place. If he didn't walk away now, everything would be ruined. And it would be all his fault.

Jori couldn't let that happen.

Sun peeked out around his bedroom's blackout curtains, but his bedside clock informed him it was far too early in the morning to be awake. Summer on Aorsa meant daylight at all hours.

If he tried, he could grab another few hours of sleep. But his hand was sticky and the memory of his dream haunted him stronger than any ghost.

Jori stood and headed for his shower. He could get in a workout before he went to work.

And then it was time to request another assignment.

2

True morning on the streets of Osais was a world removed from Jori's dreams, and he could just about pretend nothing was wrong, that his dreams and the woman at the center of them weren't determined to ruin his career.

In the distance he heard the low rumble of the factories churning out war material, but the sky was clear. He'd heard stories from Solan's human Match, Lena, that her home planet was full of pollution, skies obscured by smoke and vehicle exhaust.

It sounded like a nightmare.

If he looked the other way, the spires from the palace jutted into the sky, a reminder of his queen and what he was fighting for.

But he didn't fight for her, not really. He was as loyal as any soldier. He'd do what he was ordered. But he looked away from the castle spires and spotted a handful of children laughing and playing outside of a daycare.

That was who he fought for.

Two of the children in the group looked human. It wasn't easy to spot the difference. Zulir skin had more of a sheen to it, almost a glow, but that was more apparent in the dark. And there was the spark, of course. Humans didn't have that, not unless they were Matched with Zulir.

None of the children cared that they weren't the same. And as long as the Synnrs kept control of Aorsa, things would stay that way. If they failed, none of those human children would be playing with Zulir. The Apsyns believed that humans, all aliens, were lesser species.

He wouldn't let them spread their hate to his home.

One of the children met his eye and waved. He waved back before continuing on. If he stalled any longer, he'd be late.

He'd just stepped into the road when a rider on a fusion cycle raced by, nearly plowing straight into him.

Jori made a rude gesture and then quickly pulled it back when he remembered the children behind him. No use teaching the little ones interesting new insults.

Braznon's bowels. That rider was going to get someone killed.

But it wasn't Jori's responsibility.

His ears popped before Jori fully heard the sound, and a shockwave punched his chest. Jori moved before he fully realized what was happening, racing towards the daycare and screaming at the children to get down.

The second explosion knocked him flat on his face in the middle of the street.

Children screamed. Adults ran. Vehicles skidded and crashed.

The smoke in the air burned his lungs, but Jori pushed past it. He sprang back up and scanned the street around him.

No damage to the buildings.

No fire.

No bodies.

The bomb wasn't on this street.

He'd almost been plowed down by a biker speeding away. Whoever it was, they were long gone now, and Jori had other things to deal with, but his mind snagged on it, turning it over while he ran.

Already, the childminders were gathering the kids, so he forced himself to turn away.

He followed the path of destruction around the corner and walked into the underworld.

It was eerily silent, though several Zulir staggered down the street, one with his wings wrapped around himself in a comforting pose usually only seen in young children.

A woman huddled on the side of the street, half sitting in a puddle of liquid that Jori desperately hoped wasn't blood. His feet scuffed on the ground, the sound somehow breaking through the strange cloud of silence, and she looked up.

All he could see in her eyes was sorrow, and it was a lance through the heart.

He had nothing but basic first aid training and already could hear the emergency sirens echoing down the street. He had to do his own work, help in his own way. And that meant heading deeper into the smoke and debris.

This couldn't be good for his lungs. He'd be sent to the infirmary for sure, but if a bit of smoke inhalation was his worst injury in this war, he'd be thankful.

It was a farce to call it a war. Wars had battles. Armies fought one another.

This was a slaughter of civilians.

The roar of a fusion cycle engine cut through the smoke, and Jori saw headlights for a half a breath before the red and yellow beast ripped out of the shadows, barreling straight towards him.

He jumped to the right as the vehicle skidded left. This time, Jori gave chase, but on foot he was no match for a vehicle.

But he did make out a strange sigil on the helmet of the rider.

He'd seen something like that before at one of the bike exhibitions aficionados put on. There were clubs in the city full of men and women who swore by bikes. Who was hiding out in their ranks? In the middle of a crisis, everyone was a suspect.

Jori pulled out his communicator and sketched out the sigil to the best of his memory, even though the drawing looked like a particularly unskilled child had sketched it.

He had other skills.

And anything was better than nothing.

His communicator buzzed with an incoming call. Jori answered. Even in the middle of a war zone, he'd take a call from Major Ozar. "Where are you, Harek? We've got reports of a bombing, and you were due in my office fifteen minutes ago."

Fifteen minutes? Had it really been that long?

Time compressed in the tragedy, and Jori couldn't even say what day it was, let alone the hour.

"I'm on site, ma'am." He gave a brief assessment, including his suspicion about the biker, but there wasn't much else to tell.

"Good. Stay there. I have teams converging and want your eyes on this. We'll have to reschedule our meeting. Is there anything urgent you need to tell me?" Jori couldn't tell if she really wanted to know. The major was brusque at normal times. In a high pressure situation, her tone would be considered churlish if she had a lower rank.

And Jori had enough self-preservation to keep his issues to himself. His cock would have to deal with it for now. "No, ma'am."

On the bright side, he didn't have to face Hanna today.

But he'd face her every day for the rest of his life if he could undo the destruction all around him.

———

Another day, another interrogation. Hanna wondered what she could tell them next. Her grandmother's secret cookie recipe? That she had stolen candy from the corner store when she was six?

What crime would Jori believe?

She wore the same dark uniform she'd been wearing for weeks. Well, not completely the same. Her quarters had three versions of the same outfit that were taken away and laundered for her in rotation. She might have appreciated the service if it didn't come with a cell.

Her feet were cold in the slippers she wore. They were thin and terrible at keeping the chill out. They were also too big, and she kept having to flex her toes to keep them from slipping off.

But at least she had shoes. She'd be shivering otherwise.

The door opened and Hanna perked up, hating herself even as her body angled towards the door. Having inconvenient feelings for her interrogator was going to get her in trouble.

She was still disappointed when the man who walked through the door wasn't Jori.

He was Zulir, probably close to her age, and wearing a crisply pressed military uniform. He had short hair and a closed expression. She could see the slightest hint of a tattoo peeking out from his collar and wondered if it was a Synnr Match tattoo.

Synnrs loved to mark themselves, and Hanna

would be lying if she said she wasn't fascinated by it. But she was a spy. Lying was what she did.

Or what she used to do.

Where's Jori? The words were on the tip of her tongue, and she only barely managed to bite them back. She didn't see Jori every day. They'd never spoken outside the confines of the interrogation.

For all she knew, he was on vacation with his wife and three children.

"What's that look for?" today's interrogator asked.

Hanna realized she was scowling and schooled her expression. She shrugged. No use starting out the meeting with a lie, and she definitely wasn't going to admit she had a preference for anyone on the team. "Who are you?"

The man set a thick file on the table between them, just far enough to be out of reach. It had to be on purpose. Hanna's fingers itched to grab it and read through. What secrets did they think she was hiding?

Who was she to the Synnr military?

Who was she at all anymore?

"My name is Solan Zadra. Major Ozar asked me to talk to you." Solan took a seat and pulled the folder closer to himself but didn't open it.

Solan Zadra. There was a wealthy Zadra family on

Aorsa. He could be a member. Part of her job training had involved memorizing the richest and most influential Synnr families. Not that the information would do her any good now.

"Was letting me stew in here all morning a new trick?" She'd been brought in for interrogation not long after breakfast. Since then it had been hours, so long waiting that a guard had even brought her lunch. She'd snatched a brief glance out the door, but the interrogation room was off a hallway and she couldn't see anything important.

It was weird. She didn't like weird.

"What do you know about Starstone Construction?" He tapped his finger against the file twice before flattening his hand over it.

"Never heard of it. Is Starstone a name or a building material?" She wasn't a carpenter and had never considered having anything built. Certainly not on Aorsa. Her time on the planet was limited to her brief stint at the university.

Luci.

Punt. Hanna spent most of her days trying desperately not to think about the young woman she'd hurt. Luci was an innocent kid who'd gotten caught up in interspace politics and espionage. It had worked out alright in the end; after all, Hanna was the one in a cage while Luci was all snuggled up with her hulking Synnr warrior, but it didn't undo the damage Hanna had caused.

"What about Fazuz Realty?" Solan continued in his annoyingly terse tone. "Or the Xynthorp Taxi Company? NovaTek Toys and Robotics?"

"I think I remember seeing signs for the realty company when I was at the university, but otherwise I've never heard of these companies." A real estate agent, a toy company, a taxi service, and construction. They didn't have anything to do with each other. And they certainly had nothing to do with her.

So why ask?

Zadra flipped open the folder and pulled out a photograph before sliding it her way. "Tell me what you see."

It was low quality security camera footage of a street. Probably Osais, though she couldn't be certain. Her eyes automatically focused on the center of the image. "That's a SynStar 5, maybe a 4 if it was late model. Released about 6 years ago, it's one of the best bikes on the market. You don't see many of them on Aorsa since they need to be imported from the shop down on Kilrym, and they're ridiculously expensive, even before the export costs."

"You know a lot about this bike," he prodded, not quite coming up to the tip of an accusation.

But it made Hanna relax in her seat. "You're looking at the Sunset League under-16 Junior Fusion Cycle Champion. It should be in my file."

"It's in Hanna Karsyn's file," he agreed, and yet his tone suggested otherwise.

She groaned and put her head in her hands. At least she wasn't being handcuffed during these things anymore. "How many times do I have to tell you? I'm Hanna Karsyn. I wasn't working under a fake identity. My handler assured me that it would be fine and that my real identity would do well for the mission. There was no reason to lie."

"You planted a bomb on a university campus and stole important research."

"It wasn't a bomb and it wasn't me. The Apsyns responsible were taken into custody." She had to take a deep breath to get her heartrate under control. She'd told Jori this a dozen times, and other interrogators too. No one wanted to believe her. Time to try again. "I knew something would happen that day. It was a distraction. I hacked into an admin computer at the same time, I should be on security footage."

"You're not. You know the footage was wiped." He stood and grabbed a bottle of water from the small table behind him. "Would you like something to drink?"

"No."

Distraction. Get her riled up and then wrong-foot her. This guy knew how to ask questions. Hanna would have been concerned if she was lying.

"How many SynStar bikes would you guess are on Aorsa?" Solan asked. He made a small notation and waited for her answer.

Hanna thought for a moment. "Maybe a couple hundred. And none new this year because of the war. What's this from? What happened?"

Solan plucked the photo from her hands and put it back in his file.

Before he could say anything else, the door opened and Major Ozar stuck her head in. She was about Hanna's mother's age and had the firm expression of a career military officer. "Wrap it up, Zadra."

Solan got to his feet and gathered up the file. "I'm done here, ma'am. I'll have my report to you soon. It will be illuminating."

Hanna narrowed her eyes. She hadn't told him anything he didn't know about her. And he could have learned about the bike from anywhere. What was he playing at? Was he trying to frame her for something?

Major Ozar gave Hanna an assessing look before turning and leading Solan out of the room.

Hanna slumped back in her chair. She wasn't sure what that was all about, but she was afraid she was going to find out.

3

Jori could still feel the grit of dust and debris abrade his skin. It didn't matter that he'd showered twice already and soaked in a tub for nearly an hour. Soap and water couldn't wash away the horror of the attack.

He'd found a body.

It wasn't the first corpse he'd seen. It hadn't been particularly gruesome. The victim almost looked like he was napping, if you ignored the giant piece of metal piercing his chest.

Another restless night had him yawning as he marched into work. He'd wanted a distraction from the sweat soaked, seductive dreams of Hanna, but he'd take them back in a heartbeat. What he wanted most was this war to be over.

But even that was its own kind of cruel lie. Jori needed this war. Wars were where military careers were made and lost. If he distinguished himself, he'd come out of this with a higher rank, more responsibility, and the respect of superiors who currently didn't know his name.

"Harek!" came Major Ozar's summons.

Well. There was one superior who did know his name, and Jori wasn't sure that was a good thing. It was difficult to believe this was the woman who'd raised Oz, a fellow soldier who had an even temper and rarely said an unkind word.

Though, if he was being fair, he couldn't say the major was unkind. She was just... busy.

He hurried past desks piled with papers and around soldiers who looked like they hadn't slept in weeks, despite the fact that the explosion had only happened three days ago. He knew the feeling. He'd been working with Oz and his Match, Emily Saint, on cleanup and investigation.

The major's office was incredibly neat. The area around the desk was clear of papers and electronics, and Jori was pretty sure dust would shrivel up and disappear in fear before the major could spot it.

The only ornamentation was a small shelf with a

picture of Oz and a man Jori didn't recognize along with two medals, one bearing the royal seal.

Major Ozar nodded for him to take a seat. The chair beneath him was firm, the cushion cold beneath his fingertips.

He'd been in exactly one general's personal office, and it had been as ornate as he imagined the queen's throne room. The major rejected adornment and she didn't stand on ceremony.

Major Ozar clicked a button on her keyboard and an image was projected on the wall behind her. "We were able to identify the fusion cycle speeding away from the scene. It's a SynStar model 5.2, produced three years ago in a small factory in Vanen. Forty-seven of this model have been imported on Aorsa. We only got a partial look at the ID on the vehicle, but combined with knowledge of the model, our researchers have uncovered this man."

A second press of the button brought up an image of a middle aged Zulir man with a bushy beard, long dark hair, and a look in his eyes that spelled trouble. His gaze was fierce, eyes narrowed in defiance, and that beard of his was woven through with silver strands. The picture had probably come from an ID badge and only showed him from the shoulders up, but those shoulders were broad, and Jori imagined this guy's muscles had muscles.

"Who is he?" Not a soldier, that was for certain. This looked more like a mug shot.

"Morn Kark." The picture was replaced by a slide listing off petty crimes going back twenty years. "He owns a bar and leads his crew of troublemakers in raising havoc in their sector of the city. He was born in Osais and has never left the planet, but he's shown a troubling interest in Apsyn ideology."

"It's not a crime to think like an Apsyn," Jori said, though in the midst of a war, *that* flirted with treason.

"Of course not," Ozar agreed. "But one of the Apsyn saboteurs from the attack at the university was a regular at Kark's bar. One of his Demons."

"What?" he sputtered.

"The Rebel Demons. Mostly they drink and harass bystanders in the eastern quadrant, but a few of them have taken up the Apsyn cause. We checked Kark out after the attack, but there was nothing to pin to him. The bar has a few tax issues and noise complaints, but not out of line with any other establishment in the city. The report notes he may be an Apsyn sympathizer, but he doesn't have the funds or the motivation to do much about it."

"What's changed?" There were hundreds, maybe

thousands, of people with sympathies to the Apsyns on Aorsa. The same thing went for Synnrs on Kilrym. Before the war, travel between Kilrym and Aorsa had been free, if cautious. Now every passage was highly monitored, expensive, and dangerous.

"That's what I want you to find out." She clicked another button and the screen went blank. Then she opened a drawer, pulled out a folder, and handed it to him.

Jori scanned the summary on the front page. "Infiltration? I'm not a spy."

"No, you're not. But I need someone who understands fusion cycles."

He furrowed his brow in confusion. "I don't know much about fusion cycles either."

"Can you ride one?"

"It was part of my training, I passed the test." And it had been fun, though Ozar didn't need to know about the joy ride he and a fellow soldier, Felyx, had taken when they were supposed to be cleaning the bikes.

"Good." She sat back in her chair and didn't elaborate.

It still made no sense. "There have to be experts. And I'm still not a spy. This isn't—what's going on, Major?"

"I do have access to a fusion cycle expert who has the perfect background to infiltrate Kark's organization. But she needs backup, and I need someone I trust beyond any reasonable doubt. Someone to make sure I haven't made a mistake." She nodded towards the file. "Turn the page."

Jori's hand hovered over the paper, but he already knew who he'd see on page two. Hanna Karysn. "No. Not a chance. We can't trust her."

"My best analysts say otherwise. They were studying your reports, Harek." She held up a hand before Jori could try to contradict that. "But you have good instincts, and perhaps there's something the analyst failed to account for. That's why I want you on this mission. You see her for almost all that she is."

"Almost? What am I missing?"

"That she's an asset. If she can be trusted, she's exactly the kind of person we can use. Can I trust you on this mission?"

If Jori weren't sitting in front of his superior officer, he would have laughed. And then possibly cried. Three days ago, he'd been determined to put Hanna Karsyn in his past. She was in his head... and other places.

He could tell Ozar his judgement was compromised. She'd pull him from the mission then.

But would she still send Hanna in? What if Hanna betrayed them? Who would have her back?

What if she got hurt?

He was an idiot for even considering taking the mission. But Ozar was depending on him.

And so was Hanna.

If he did this right, his career could get just the boost he was looking for.

He tried to hold that reason close. It was logical. It was correct.

And it was utter bullshit.

"When do we start?"

———

Second chances didn't come every day, and Hanna had been waiting for hers for more than a month. She could imagine one of the priestesses back home chiding her for impatience, but the temple of the gods in Vanen was way nicer than Hanna's cell, so the priestess could shut up.

Hanna rubbed her wrists but jerked her hands apart when she realized she was doing it. She wasn't cuffed. She wasn't in a cell. No one was guarding her. She was free.

Almost.

There had to be a guard somewhere in this giant building. And she would bet he was under orders to not let her walk away. But she wouldn't. She finally could be useful.

She was trying not to think too hard about who she was being useful for. Yes, Hanna had defected. After seeing what the Apsyns were willing to do to win the war, she'd had no other choice. Helping that side would be monstrous. They wanted to rip apart Matched Zulir units as if it wouldn't destroy something sacred. Hanna couldn't stand for it.

But her parents were still in Vanen. Her school friends. People she'd known her entire life. And her actions...

No. If she did this right, they'd be even safer. Because she was going to help end the war. Then no one would have to suffer anymore.

Besides, her choice had been simple: rot in her cell forever or assist on an undercover mission. If it went well, she wouldn't get sent back to the cell. Hanna was going to make sure she ended this job a free woman.

Even if it meant running at the first opportunity and living in a cave for the rest of her life.

She shuddered at the thought. Caves had bugs. And mold. And bears. Not ideal for a city girl like her.

Pacing from one end of the bench she was supposed

to be sitting on to the other, Hanna studied the warehouse around her. Most of it was obscured by shadow. The lights were high in the ceiling, and only the set over the benches had been turned on. But she could make out ramps and stairs and the outlines of alcoves.

This was a training facility. She flared her wings out and relaxed into the stretch. They weren't physical things, but she always felt freer when she displayed them. Her spark and her wings were a part of her, and she embraced it.

When was her partner supposed to get here? And who was she working with? She'd asked Solan when he laid out the mission for her, but he hadn't said. Apparently details were still being worked out. Those details had left her stranded here, eager to do something but unsure of what.

She knew the basics of the mission. She and a Synnr partner would be infiltrating a fusion cycle gang of Apsyn sympathizers. The Synnrs wanted her for her bike knowledge and skills. Hanna was happy to play the part. She missed the purr of a bike under her as she ate up miles of open road.

A door on the far side of the room opened, blasting bright light into the dim room and haloing the Synnr who walked in.

Jori.

Hanna's body had a weird reaction to that, heart pounding fast, skin prickling with awareness, and the rest of her unsure of whether to be wary or turned on. Hanna had spent a lot of time looking at Jori Harek. There wasn't much else to do when he did those interrogation sessions that were really just staring contests.

He was a lithe man, and a bit short for a Zulir male. If they stood next to one another, they'd be the same height. He had curly hair that he sometimes held back with a plain black headband or tons of styling product. The first time Hanna had seen it, she'd been tempted to blow up her entire future just so she could reach out and touch it.

And his eyes... they were something her mother had warned her about. The kind of eyes that only needed one look to get a person into bed. Dark, mysterious, and oh so sensual. That sensuality was only challenged for supremacy by his lips.

She wanted to taste him. She wanted to feel the scruff of his beard against her skin as they rolled around in his bed and did all the wicked things she wasn't supposed to think about.

There was an intensity to the Synnr that made the

sensuality all the more tempting. What did he look like when he fell apart?

What did his wings look like?

She'd never seen them. Synnrs seemed less likely to put theirs on display, and she'd received more than a few strange looks for leaving hers exposed. But that was a part of herself Hanna refused to hide.

As Jori got close enough, the first thing he did was stare at her wings. Hanna flicked them, not enough to make it obvious, but in a move she knew drew attention to the vein of black that ran through the center.

Jori jerked his gaze away and looked square at her forehead as if he couldn't bear to look her in the eye. "You've been briefed?"

"Are you my partner?" Stupid! Why would she even ask that? What else could he be, meeting with her in this training facility? "And, yes, I've been briefed. But I'm not sure what we're doing here."

"Training." The word came out as dry as day old toast.

"Yes, thank you. I could work that part out. I meant specifically. If we do this right, we shouldn't be fighting. When I—" she cut herself off. No need to remind the man of her past, even if there was no way to forget.

Jori stared at that same spot on her forehead for several long seconds, waiting for her to finish.

Hanna kept her mouth shut.

Eventually he let out a breath. "This is for team building. The covert team is finalizing our backstories right now, but sitting in a room and memorizing files isn't going to do much for selling our... relationship." He had to swallow past something in his throat to get that word out. We're going to run the course as a team."

She nodded and scanned over the parts of the course she could see. "Sounds fun."

He made a sound of frustration. "It's not fun, Miss Karsyn. This is life and death."

"What's the point of life if you don't have a little fun? And the name's Hanna, Jori. You're going to blow our cover if you forget that."

Their gazes met, and it had to be a trick of the light, but Hanna could swear that she saw Jori's spark dancing in his eyes. Could she have riled him up that much just by saying his name?

Deep in the warehouse she heard something slam shut, then the light over the door behind her flicked from blue to yellow.

"Did we just get locked in?"

"It's part of the mission. We're supposed to work

together to find the controller for the doors and unlock them. We're stuck here until we do." The lights were starting to come on, still dim, but giving her enough illumination to see the true breadth of the course.

"*Obviously* we're both awesome and will kill this course in no time, but what if we can't find the controls? Or if there's a fire?"

Hanna had to be hallucinating. She could have sworn she saw a smile tug at his cheek, but it was gone in a second. "Obviously the locks disengage if there's an emergency. And the doors will automatically disengage in six hours if we fail."

Six hours stuck in a warehouse alone with Jori. Hanna wasn't sure if that was a fantasy come true or a nightmare.

Jori nodded towards the edge of the course. "Follow me."

4

THIS WAS NEVER GOING to work.

Hanna pushed herself up from where Jori had pushed her down—to avoid an obstacle, he assured her—and glared at her partner. Sweat dripped down her back and exhaustion made her bones heavy.

How long had they been doing this? Two hours? Four?

She feared that if she had a watch, she'd find out they hadn't been on the course for more than thirty minutes.

Jori was a harsh taskmaster and he didn't want to hear a word from her that wasn't *yessir*. Hanna's spark sizzled in her veins, and it had nothing to do with his sultry good looks or strokable hair.

"Do it again," Jori ordered as he watched her slowly push herself to her feet. And, of course, he didn't offer a hand up. At this point, Hanna would have batted it away.

"We've been stuck here for a while. Your way isn't working. We need to double back." They were stuck between two small towers on the course. In front of them, a large pendulum swung back and forth, cutting them off from jumping between one tower and the next. Even more frustrating, if they approached the edge of the tower and hesitated for more than a second, a hovering drone blasted at them.

Thus the tackle.

"This is the way forward," Jori insisted. "I've done this course before."

"And if you don't think that there are multiple ways to complete a course like this, you're crazy." She backed up to the far edge of the tower and eyed the ladder that would lead her back to the ground.

The course was all sharp edges and dark corners. And it was chock full of drones and robots ready to challenge them if they turned the wrong corner or ducked into the wrong alcove.

"The controls are in the box on the next tower," Jori told her, reaching for her but stopping his hand before they actually made contact. He only seemed willing to touch her if he was violently tackling her to the floor.

"Then let's get there another way." Hanna was tired of failing. And, frankly, listening to Jori was going to drive her insane. "You're doing this too... straightforwardly."

"What?" He glared at her before turning back to the pendulum. He rushed the edge and paused, darting back as the drone came into sight. "It's a straightforward challenge."

"Maybe for a soldier, but we're not soldiers right now, Jori. We have to think creatively." Something below them crashed, and Hanna glanced down. "*Punt.*"

"What is it?"

She shot a burst of her spark down the ladder. "There's a robot trying to climb up. We're stuck here."

"Fine," Jori spat, like the word was a curse. "You want to do it like a *punting* spy, give it a shot."

His attitude on clandestine work was going to be an issue, but Hanna pushed it to the back of her mind. She breathed out her worries and found her center. She couldn't deal with the robot, it wasn't a problem yet. She needed to get to the other tower and grab those keys, and then they could go home.

She crept forward, crouched low, and eyed the

structure beside the tower. There. It looked like a rivet, but it was out of alignment, just a smidge. She was betting it was the sensor that triggered the drone.

Hanna summoned her spark and aimed, lashing out in a controlled blast that seared the sensor and made the drone shrilly beep for three seconds before it fell out of the sky.

One obstacle down.

Hanna flared out her wings. Zulir couldn't fly, but they could glide a little. The second tower was a bit lower than the one she was standing on. She was pretty sure she could make the jump. But once she leapt, there was no coming back for Jori.

She came back to herself just enough to hear the sounds of a struggle behind her. He was fighting the robot, which had managed to get up the ladder and was trying to get onto the roof. Jori had the upper hand, but if the robot got all the way up, he wouldn't stand a chance.

Too bad.

Hanna timed her jump, waiting until the pendulum was in the middle of its swing. She spread her wings and fell.

Hanna glided past the pendulum and landed on the lower platform with too much speed. She had to take a couple of steps to slow herself down, and even then, she still crashed into the wall at the back of the landing.

"Jori, get your ass over here!" They were almost home free, they just needed to finish this.

She examined the pedestal that contained the controls. Nothing special about that. Hanna tried to open the box on top, but there was a small lock. She forced it open with her spark.

Yellow lights flashed, sirens blared, and the lights came back on as a voice over the speaker announced: "Mission failed. Exit the training field and prepare to reset."

Hanna glared down at the locked box. Was it her spark? How had she messed up?

Then she looked back toward the platform where Jori was supposed to be and saw him pinned under the robot. It had a blaster pointed at his head but removed it after a moment, backed away from him, and made its way to the corner of the platform.

"I thought you had that!" Hanna yelled across the distance. She looked for a ladder or stairs, but didn't see any. She flared her wings and jumped off, gliding down to the floor, feet sinking into the padding around the structure.

Jori took two bounding steps and leapt, flaring his wings at the last second. Hanna's breath caught at the display. Mostly blue, with highlights of white and darker blue, his wings were a thing of beauty. And the second he landed, he pulled them back in. His face was a wash of anger as he stalked past her.

"What happened?" Hanna asked. "I was seconds away from breaking into the box."

He let out a growl of frustration but didn't look at her. He stopped at the edge of the training field where there was a screen mounted to the wall, and started scrolling through menus.

"Talk to me." She didn't like to fail, and she liked the silent treatment even less.

Jori whipped around, spark dancing in his eyes and anger making his voice harsh. "It's a teamwork mission, Apsyn. What did you think would happen when you abandoned me to face a bot that takes two people to defeat?"

"And I was supposed to know that how?" She stepped close, got up in his space, and matched his glare with her own. "You spent the entire time we were up there shouting orders as if I was your lackey. We're supposed to be partners. Equals. You're supposed to listen to me too."

"You're a spy." There was vitriol there, but his eyes flicked down to her lips, just for a moment.

Oh. Oh no. It was one thing for her to have an inconvenient... awareness... of the Synnr. It couldn't be reciprocated. That way led to disaster.

And if her heart was beating a little faster, she'd blame it on the exercise. It had nothing to do with Jori.

"Ex-spy. Ex. And why do you have anything against spies? They're just as important as soldiers."

Now he scoffed. "Because a knife in the dark kills all the same?"

"I've never assassinated anyone." She wasn't proud of everything she'd done in her short-lived espionage career, but that wasn't a mark she had to clean away.

Jori's chest heaved, but he turned back to the screen. "This isn't working."

"Maybe if we actually make an effort to work together..." But he wasn't listening.

This job was going to get them both killed.

"Training parameters altered," said a computerized voice when Jori took a step back.

"What's that? I thought you said we're locked in here until the training is done?" She wanted to elbow him out of the way to see what he'd changed on the screen, but touching him right now, when her awareness was at an all time high, seemed... not smart.

"We can't unlock the doors," he confirmed, "but we can change the training. You want to show me what you've got, now it's your turn. We're going one on one. The lockboxes are being moved, the drones and robots repositioned." A small slot opened under the screen and spat out a handful of papers. Jori held them out to her. "Here are your prep docs. You have ten minutes. Once the warning bell sounds, we begin."

"That's not what..." She trailed off. Jori wasn't going to listen to reason. He wanted to play?

Game on.

———

Jori loved training in the obstacle field. His mind snagged on all the twists and turns thrown his way, working the problems until it all transformed into a puzzle that only he could solve.

If Major Ozar read the training report, she would curse him to Braznon's bowels for changing the mission, but she was a busy woman. And if he had to work with the spy for another minute, the training center might descend into bloodshed.

He could do the job, even if he had to do it with her. But not this course. She couldn't come into his favorite place to train and leave her mark on it. He wouldn't allow it.

He'd walked into the second mission ready to crush her. He'd run a dozen variants of this course and knew that other soldiers dreaded fighting him in here. He didn't give up. And mercy? That had no place.

But Hanna didn't know his reputation, and her eyes had lit with anticipation as she scanned over the mission parameters.

He shouldn't have been looking. He had his own prep to do, but whenever she was close, his eyes found her. It was involuntary.

And deadly.

He didn't trust her. He didn't trust any spy, not even the ones working for his side. He couldn't count on her. And getting distracted? It was a death sentence.

Jori pulled his focus back to the mission. They were both on the course now, set up at their starting positions. Their prep documents had each included a crude map with their target circled. Jori didn't have an advantage of knowing the layout, as it shifted with every mission to suit the needs of the trainees.

He might not have known the twists and turns,

but he knew the obstacles, the drones, and the bots that patrolled, ready to wreak havoc.

And the other treats.

The final signal rang, their cue to move. Jori jumped into action. He wasn't sure where Hanna was, but he got a hint when he heard a flurry of curses coming from somewhere north of him.

Hesitation at the start never worked. The starting positions were lined with lasers that began shooting within ten seconds if a soldier didn't haul ass.

But the initial curses died down and Jori couldn't further pinpoint Hanna's position. It couldn't matter. If he did this right, he wouldn't have to face her at all. He could get in, get the keys, and call this farce of a training mission off.

As if he'd be that lucky. These missions were designed to pit soldiers against one another, to truly test their skills. Avoiding his opponent would be impossible.

That was, if the course didn't get to him first. Electricity buzzed in front of him, a live wire that was one of the most dangerous obstacles in the room. Not enough to kill a person, but getting hit by it would make him wish he was cursed to *braz*.

Jori wanted to run. He wanted to bound up one of the ramps to get a better view of his surroundings, but drones flew overhead and Hanna was somewhere. He had to stay out of sight for as long as he could.

He heard a sharp intake of breath to his left and lashed out with his spark before he had a chance to confirm it was her. Everyone and everything in this challenge was unfriendly.

Hanna grunted and flew back into the wall where the live wire danced overhead. Her wings flashed out, making her an even bigger target. If she was a soldier, he would have reamed her out for the lack of discipline.

But her mistake was his advantage.

Her left wing dipped and he anticipated her next move, dodging away before her kick connected. But he didn't see her spark coming, not until her electricity was racing up his chest and sinking deep into him.

Something felt... off about that. It should have hurt, should have left him staggering. Instead he almost felt like he'd absorbed the energy.

An Apsyn trick. Surely.

"What—" Hanna's question was cut off when a drone caught their movement and swooped in.

Jori sprinted away, leaving her to fight just as she'd abandoned him in the previous mission. He needed to head southeast, but landmarks were difficult to come by. With Hanna distracted, he used the opportunity to climb one of the platforms and get a look at his surroundings.

There. He couldn't see his target, but there was a temple spire that marked the correct direction. He jumped from one platform to the next, covering even more ground and only needing to backtrack once to avoid a drone hovering off the edge of one of the platforms.

Victory was in his grasp. Hanna was probably still stuck fighting that drone.

He wouldn't celebrate victory before it was his.

Jori had to carefully climb down from the platform he was perched on. The lockbox had moved from its previous position. Now, instead of a platform, it was sunken into a recess in the floor, nearly two meters deep. Easy to get to, but he'd be a defenseless target for whatever guarded the keys.

He needed a distraction.

He needed Hanna. If he threw her in, the security measures would target her and let him go on his merry way.

She had the same idea. His only warning was a footstep behind him before a kick landed straight in his back, sending him sprawling, but not quite over the ledge into the pit.

"Are you made of cement?" Hanna demanded as

she dodged away. Her wings were out again and Jori had to ignore them, even as part of him wanted to admire their beauty. The variance in their color, the depth of them—it wasn't something you saw every day.

He shot his spark her way before he could get too lost in admiration. Hanna grunted but didn't go down.

"How are you doing that?" she demanded.

"If you haven't learned how to use your spark, we're both dead." She was trying to distract him. Playing dirty. And he was falling for it. No more responses, he promised himself. They didn't need to talk to fight.

He shot out his spark again, missing her, but it gave him cover to rush in close and sweep her legs, sending her backwards into the pit.

Hanna screamed as she fell and somehow managed to right herself and latch onto the edge of the pit. Her scream of surprise turned to terror and pain, and Jori paused.

Nothing in the obstacle course could kill them.

But accidents in training happened all the time.

"It's got me, Jori!" Her words were sheer terror. "It hurts. Oh *braz* it hurts. Help!"

He was at war with himself, but he'd never

heard someone fake such desperation before. Jori rushed in and reached for her hand. "Come on, I've got you."

They could always reset.

Hanna made a sound of gratitude, but her breathing didn't even. Instead of taking his hand, she clamped onto his wrist.

And that was when Jori knew he'd been had.

She put her entire bodyweight into it and tugged him down into the pit with her, twisting in the air until he was the one that landed flat on his back as the air was knocked out of him.

Dirty Apsyn spy.

Hanna straddled his waist and grinned down at him, her hand clamped over the wrist she'd grabbed. "Aren't you the gentleman, Jori Harek?" Her words were a caress and a knife.

He arched against her, trying to buck her off, but she had leverage. And his body liked the feel of her far too much. His blood was pumping, adrenaline flowing through his veins, and he was helpless to stop the reaction.

If she felt the thick press of his cock, she didn't show it, and that was its own small mercy.

With her free hand, Hanna reached into a pocket on her uniform and pulled out a strange black device.

It took Jori a second to realize that it was the laser housing from the drone she'd fought.

She aimed it at the sensor on his chest and pressed a button.

"Oh, too bad." She gave him an exaggerated frown. "Looks like you're dead."

She stood up and slid the laser device back into her pocket. Jori struggled to get up, but they were both wearing harnesses designed to track the damage they accrued during the mission. When the sensors said they were dead, they were more or less frozen in place until the mission ended.

Hanna moved carefully through the pit, using her spark and the laser to cut through the security measures until she made it to the box holding the door controls.

He watched as she flipped it open and pressed the button that ended the exercise and unlocked the doors.

The pressure from his vest disappeared as if it had never been there, and he got to his feet.

Hanna turned towards him with a bright grin. "I win."

"You cheated." That scream would haunt his nightmares. "That was a dirty spy trick." How could he ever trust her when she pulled stunts like that?

"I. Won." She stalked his way and traced a finger down the center of his chest. "You need to get over this spy stuff. We're going undercover. We're going to lie. And if your principles get me killed, I will hunt you through the darkest recesses of *braz* until your soul begs for the darkness of undoing." She patted his chest before walking away, leaving Jori alone in the pit with the sinking suspicion that she had a point.

5

Hanna stormed into the locker room ready to hit something. Anything.

No, not anything.

If she was going to hit anyone, he was standing back in the training room with that angry look on his face. As if he had some moral high ground for his job. They were both pawns.

She yanked off the sensor vest and let it fall to the floor. The rest of her clothes quickly followed before she marched to the shower and turned the water to scalding, as if that could burn out the memory of Jori's hate.

But it wasn't the anger that made her blood sing. Or not only the anger. There'd been a moment back there, after she had the better of him, straddling his thighs and grinning down at him, that all she could think of was what that might be like if they weren't in a training mission.

If they were in his bed.

Hanna groaned and knocked her fist against the slick tile wall.

Admiring him was bad when there was that interrogation table between them. But it was... controllable. That table was a sure sign that nothing could happen, a gap as wide as a vast canyon.

But the table was gone now. And she knew what the press of his body felt like, even if it only came in fleeting bursts in the middle of the mission.

She had to put it out of her mind. How she was going to do that when they were about to start a job that would have them in each other's pockets at all hours, she wasn't sure.

At least the day was almost over.

Hanna took her time showering. She'd had access to facilities when she was under lock and key, but a guard had always been standing just out of sight. Now she had true privacy. It didn't change much about how she soaped herself up, but some tension bled out from between her shoulders.

The soap in the facility canister smelled clean, but mass produced with a slightly astringent undernote.

It reminded her more of dish soap than anything else, but luckily it didn't leave her skin unbearably dry.

The towel was also mass produced, an over-washed white that was too thin to be truly absorbent, but big enough to engulf her when she wrapped it around herself. These were both reminders that she was tied up in a military op. Plentiful decent products, but not a luxury to be seen.

Nothing to get hung up on.

There was a change of clothes waiting for Hanna and beside it, a vehicle keycode and an address. Her new home. They were trusting her to get there on her own.

How nice.

The address didn't tell her much, but beside the clothes and papers there was a communicator. She used the device to pull up a map around the address and nodded to herself.

She'd lived in Osais for a couple of months for her last job, establishing her identity as a university student. She was familiar with the area around the university and its trendy shops and cool vibe.

Her new home was on the other side of town and might as well have been in a different world. She'd studied the city before moving and had a vague knowledge of its quadrants and larger neighborhoods.

She was moving to a mostly industrial area with rough bars and rougher residents.

The perfect place for a fusion cycle gang to flourish.

Her identity wasn't anything special. She'd be going in under her own name and with a similar backstory. Hanna Karsyn, university dropout, Apsyn displaced by the war, missing home and...

Punt.

And in a romantic relationship with Jori Harek, dissatisfied Synnr soldier.

She wasn't surprised. That was how she knew she had worked it out in the back of her mind, even if the rest of her thoughts had been studiously ignoring it. It made sense. No way would the Synnrs send her in alone, not when she could ruin the entire op. But getting two people in separately would raise suspicions.

But a new biker and his woman? No one would question that.

And it would keep her close enough to Jori to help him cover for any gaps in his knowledge of fusion bikes.

Hanna read over that part of the brief again, just to make sure she wasn't missing anything. This time it didn't come as a shock.

Well. Pretending she was attracted to her partner wasn't going to be an issue. She could use what she was already feeling to sell the job. As for Jori... she didn't know how strongly he was lying to himself, but she trusted him to play his part, no matter how much he claimed to hate spies and all they stood for.

She used her communicator to scan a code on the document. It sent an encrypted digital version to her so that she could study it further later. Paper documents wouldn't leave the training facility.

Hanna needed to get out, to feel the wind in her hair and the freedom that the road could bring her.

Before she left, she put her documents in a small slot to be incinerated, just as the instructions told her. Then she was out of the building. She didn't look around for Jori. If she looked, she might see him. And if she saw him, they might have to talk.

No, walking quickly with blinders on was the best option for now.

No one tried to stop her. A guard even pointed her to the right vehicle lot.

And there was her baby.

It was a beauty of a fusion cycle and Hanna had to pause and admire it. Nothing about it screamed military issue, something she'd been vaguely concerned about.

Instead she was looking at a three or four year old Fusion Runner. The body was mostly black, with a magenta line running down each side. Both wheels had magenta accents in the wheel wells, and the seat was studded with gold bolts. It was feminine and powerful and everything she would have wanted as a young racer.

Hanna ran her fingers over the cool metal of the body and sighed in joy. This was a thing of beauty.

The controls ran along the side of the battery casing in the center of the bike. Hundreds of years ago these bikes had external handlebars, but the design had fallen out of favor when gyroscopic controls were perfected.

Hanna opened the storage hatch and pulled out a black helmet with magenta stripes, perfectly matched to the bike. If she knew the city a little better, she might risk leaving the helmet behind, but it was too dangerous.

Maybe she could take a gentle ride in the country-side before the job was done. And maybe if she was really lucky, she'd convince the powers that be to let her keep the bike after the mission.

She climbed on and engaged the motor before pressing herself against the body of the bike. Some preferred riding while sitting straight up, but

Hanna liked to feel her vehicle as she made every move.

She knew where she was supposed to be going, but instead of making her way for the thoroughfare that would take her to her new home district, Hanna turned towards the giant park in the middle of Osais. She couldn't ride fast, but the trees and green spaces were enough to let her pretend she was back home, if only for a few minutes.

She passed a group of children who pointed at her as she drove by. Hanna blew a kiss and kept moving.

Part of her was tempted to drive until the battery died. She could be hundreds of kilometers away from the city by then, out in one of the little outposts that wasn't much of a town. Hide out. Make a little life for herself. Forget Hanna Karsyn had ever existed.

But there was probably a tracking device on the bike. And Hanna wasn't made for a small town.

She took another lap around the park before pulling out onto a street that would take her towards the highway. There was never much traffic in Osais, so at least she could go fast. The bike hummed under her, and Hanna remembered her victories from those long ago competitions.

Nothing beat winning.

But the simple joy of riding came really close.

The beautiful buildings of the old town gave way to residential towers and then older houses. And beyond that were the factories that kept the moon functioning.

The air was a bit grittier out here, even if carbon scrubbers did their best to keep pollution to a minimum.

Wooden row houses lined the street, most of them seemingly held up by nothing more than pride. There were gaps between a few, buildings that had collapsed and were nothing more than empty pits or piles of rubble.

A few Synnrs sat on the steps outside of one of the houses and watched Hanna as she rode down the street. Were they calculating what they could get for the bike?

Maybe she was being rude. Just because they were poor didn't mean they were thieves.

All the same, she hoped there was ample storage for her ride.

Her new home was one street over, and the degradation of the other block hadn't spread this far yet. Two of the yards had flowers blooming in careful plots. Children played in another yard, though they were using sticks for toys. Most of the houses needed fresh coats of paint, but none had fallen down. The worst she could see was a couple of boarded up windows.

It would be fine. She hadn't expected to be staying at the palace.

She pulled onto the gravel driveway of her address and spotted a small storage shed in the back. Her bike could go there later. Hanna wouldn't forget all of her training just because she'd switched sides. She was examining a new building, and until she was absolutely sure it was safe, she wasn't storing her getaway vehicle.

She entered the entry code into the keypad lock and stepped inside.

And found Jori sitting at the kitchen table, pointing a blaster at her face.

6

Jori'd been on tough missions before. One involved living in a swamp, in the *actual* swamp, not in some shack on the water, and he'd gladly trade places with his past self.

At least there he'd never been tempted to kiss the giant people-eating reptiles that called that terrain home.

He shouldn't have been surprised when Hanna walked in the front door. Pointing the weapon? Not a good look. But he'd spent the hours before that burying himself in data about the Rebel Demons.

Theft. Smuggling. Prostitution. Murder. Links to dozens upon dozens of crimes, but only a few charges had ever stuck. Morn Kark was clever and unafraid to get his own hands dirty.

With those thoughts swirling in his mind, Jori had been a bit... jumpy.

Luckily, Hanna didn't hold that against him.

Over the last week, he'd discovered that she was an okay roommate. She didn't hog the bathroom. She left the kitchen tidy. When they weren't going over strategy for the job, she kept to herself.

And it was driving Jori nuts.

He certainly hadn't dealt with inconvenient erections while fighting off swamp creatures.

He wished he could say it was all some grand scheme by the evil Apsyn spy. But he didn't think Hanna even realized she was doing it. The row house was small, their quarters tight. And that meant they sometimes got a bit too close for comfort.

Passing each other in the hallway that led to the bedroom? Torture.

The bedroom?

He might actually die.

The house had two bedrooms, but there was only a bed in one of them. The other was filled with storage equipment and a small office space. He understood why. They were going in as a romantic couple. If, for any reason, someone from Kark's crew came to their place, they needed to play the part.

But Jori was sleeping on the couch.

It was too short for him and had an uncomfortable spring that poked into his back, but he wouldn't sleep a wink if he stayed in that bed with Hanna. Going into the room to grab a change of clothes was enough to send his thoughts spiraling somewhere they couldn't go. If they were sharing a bed...

He only had so much control.

Hanna seemed unbothered. And he was caught between annoyance and relief. A nasty part of him that he tried to keep buried wanted her suffering from this undeniable want just as much as he did. But a bigger part, a better part, was grateful that he wasn't making things impossible.

He had reasons for disliking Hanna Karsyn. He didn't want her anywhere near this job or the Synnr military. But those things were professional. He didn't want her thinking she was under some kind of... personal threat from him.

He would never take things that far.

So he suffered alone.

"Did you ride today?" The ground floor of their house contained the kitchen, where Hanna stood, with a small alcove big enough for their table, and a living area. The second floor had the bedrooms and bathroom. They even had a flat roof that could be converted into some kind of outdoor living space, but neither of them had spent much time up there.

"I did a tour of the neighborhood. A few of the tougher men saw me." This part of the job was teeth-grindingly tedious. They had to establish themselves in the neighborhood. If they showed up at Kark's place when no one had ever heard of them, they might as well announce their true plans.

"What's the design flaw of the SynStar Class 2.7?" She came out of the kitchen and sat at the table with a steaming bowl of soup.

"I don't really think I'll blow my cover by not knowing esoteric fusion bike details." He could ride adequately. He knew the ins and outs of his own bike. "This is a gang of saboteurs, not gearheads. They'll be more impressed if I tell them where to get bomb materials."

Her spoon clattered to the table and she glared at him. "The 2.7 flaw isn't esoteric. A short in the onboard battery led to catastrophic system failure, and if it happened while the bike was operational, that meant explosions. One took out an entire bridge in Vanen thirty years ago. The accident nearly killed my dad, but luckily it wasn't his bike. I'm not asking you to know all the little idiosyncrasies of these beasts."

Jori didn't respond. He could imagine the reaming Major Ozar would give him for treating Hanna's portion of this job like it was unimportant. "If they try to trip me up, I'll tell them you got me into bikes."

She gave him a skeptical look. "A guy like Kark won't take kindly to a man admitting ignorance, especially in deference to a woman." But she picked her spoon back up and ate her soup. "I passed by the bar last night."

"What?" It was vehement, and the jolt of adrenaline had Jori aching for a fight.

But Hanna ignored that. "There's a market on the same street. It's where I got the soup. I didn't go inside, I'm not an idiot. But a girl was posting a help wanted flyer on the window as I passed."

"Ozar said she'd have the police detain their bartender. Did you talk to the girl?"

"I bumped into her and introduced myself. You're right. It's a bartender position. I told her I was up from Kilrym and stranded. She got called inside before I could say much more. Her name was Zilly."

Jori mentally reviewed his files on the bar. "I think that's Kark's girl. All we know is she's been around the bar for a year or so. No criminal record. Paper thin background."

Hanna raised her eyebrows. "You think it's fake?"

He shrugged. "Could be. Or she could be an innocent girl caught up in something far bigger than herself."

"She's cute." There was something in her tone that Jori couldn't decipher.

"What's that supposed to mean?" he asked cautiously.

"It means she's cute. Why does it have to mean anything else?" She placed her spoon in her empty soup bowl and pushed it towards the center of the table. "We should go for a ride."

"What?" If he could barely keep up with a simple conversation, he had no idea how he and Hanna would pull this job off.

"You say you're good, I believe you. But I want to see it. Once I make initial contact, it's game on. And I can't see you ride for the first time when we're already in it. Besides, I've got a few showy tricks I can teach you. They're nothing to do, once you know them. But they might come in handy."

His sense of self-preservation was screaming at him to say no. But that sense had nothing to do with the job. This was exactly why Hanna was here. She could help him sell his role.

"Give me a few minutes and I'll meet you outside," he said. "I know a good place."

Hanna nodded. "I can't wait to see what you've got."

———

"Aren't you getting your bike out?" Jori asked after he locked up the back door.

Hanna ran her hand over his bike and patted the passenger seat. "If a man wants to show off for his girl, he doesn't let her ride her own bike." It was true, and also a complete lie. Hanna could follow Jori on her own bike and easily assess how he was doing.

But she didn't want to do that.

She'd been living in the same house with him for a week and it was driving her crazy. He had this way of looking at her that made her want to climb him like a mountain. She'd been in a constant state of arousal and anxiety since she walked through the door that first day, and if something didn't break one way or another, she would...

Well. She wasn't sure what she'd do. Whatever it was, she couldn't put the job at risk. That meant finding someone else was off the table for now. And climbing Jori?

The avalanche of disaster that would bring would almost be worth it.

Today Hanna was trying to give her body a tiny taste of what it wanted and hoping it would sate the gnawing need within her, as if a single bite could ever cure starvation.

Jori just shrugged, put his helmet on, and climbed on the bike.

She couldn't get a read on him. That day in the training center, she'd been so sure he was as close to desire and immolation as she was. Since then, he'd been a brick wall. Either he was an expert at hiding his emotions, or everything she felt was one sided.

One of those was better for the job. But she really didn't want to be in this alone.

She put her helmet on and climbed on behind him, pressing her body tight to his and savoring the contact. They were both covered in multiple layers, from their helmets all the way down to their riding boots. He couldn't touch anywhere sensitive, not with so much fabric between them.

And still she wanted to shiver.

Jori started the bike and Hanna realized just how terrible of an idea this truly was. The vibration of the bike under them was stimulating enough to heat her blood. Jori's body was hot and hard beneath her hands. She was tempted to wrap her arms tight around him and squeeze until there wasn't a molecule of space between them.

Instead, she kept her grip loose. There was an etiquette to being a passenger on a fusion bike, and even a tidal wave of lust couldn't stop a lifetime of training.

Jori picked up speed once they were away from residential streets and climbing an empty road to the canyon outside the city. The world whipped by in a blur of colors, the wind carrying the scents of the city and sunlight and hope. And then there was Jori, of course—this close she couldn't escape his scent, something dark and masculine. Was it cologne? Or him? It melded with the leather of his jacket, something woodsy that reminded her of a campfire.

Hanna relished it as she leaned into the curves of the road, thrilling at the feel of Jori against her as they moved together in a sensual dance of power and speed.

He might not have had much experience with the bike, but he handled it like a natural. He didn't hesitate to take sharp curves or speed up a hill. And he weaved around obstacles like they weren't there at all. He could pull this job off, alright. But she refused to think any more of that right now, not when she could live in this moment.

This was the joy of biking. Wind whipping around. The world melting away. And a partner in the dance.

"Take us on the canyon road," she told Jori through the mic in their helmets. Her face was pressed against his back, her lips nearly moving against his jacket as she spoke. "Show me what you can really do."

Jori answered her by speeding up to the edge, and then they were hurtling along the canyon road. The curves came one after another, and the unmoving sun was their only companion.

For a moment, Hanna felt free. Unencumbered. Jori's heat was pressed tight against her, a reminder of all her responsibilities and risk—if she let that reminder in.

But he was also a temptation, the one thing she couldn't resist. The one man who lit her up inside without even trying.

Her spark danced in her veins and she let her wings flash out, spreading them wide and quickly pulling them in before she affected their ride. Zulir wings didn't have true mass. They were made of electricity and controlled by the mind. But they could still catch the wind, and Zulir could glide from high to low in controlled falls.

Spreading her wings on a high speed ride might be just enough to make them crash.

She didn't care. Jori had control of the bike, and she trusted him to keep her safe.

That was the most reckless thing she'd ever done. It was impossible to do anything else when she was on the back of his bike.

He pulled the bike off the road once they reached the canyon's edge. They were on an outcropping. Any further and they'd fall off the cliff and into the canyon and the river that ran through it. Hanna was a little tempted to take two sprinting steps and leap. She was almost sure Jori would follow after her.

But the canyon was deep, and she wasn't sure her wings would keep her safe.

She swung her leg off the bike and grinned at Jori, energy thrumming through her. He grinned right back and stood.

Close.

Oh so close.

Their eyes met. Gazes locked. The grin slowly slid off her face as she watched Jori's spark dance in his eyes. She needed to say something now, anything that would break the moment and allow sanity to return.

Jori pulled his helmet off and placed it on the bike without looking away.

Hanna did the same, even as her survival instincts screamed at her to look away. But she couldn't. He might as well have chained her to him. Except this chain was made of desire.

Her body was alight with it, shivery and wet and oh so tempting to give into. Especially when Jori reached out and ran his fingers over her cheek.

She needed to pull away. One of them needed to be sane.

Why wasn't it her?

Why did it have to be her?

She leaned into the touch and knew it was all over.

This was a fight that she couldn't win. And why would she want to?

Jori leaned forward and Hanna met him. All she could do was savor the kiss that she longed for, full of teeth and tongue and a gentle caress of lips that shouldn't have felt like home.

His desire was raw and urgent. Her pussy clenched in response, wanting more, craving a deeper connection. That was a madness she couldn't surrender to, no matter how deep the need.

He drew her in and ran his hands down her back, pulling her closer until she felt every inch of him, hard and hot and so very good. The clothes between them now were a delicious torture, and they did nothing to hide the thick, hard length of him.

It wouldn't take anything to reach down, find the clasp of his pants, and free him for her touch.

Nothing but a streak of self-destruction that not even Hanna could touch.

Jori pulled away, and she tried to chase his kiss. His gaze was searching and intense, and she was sure this was the moment it ended.

She tried not to show the wave of despair that washed over her at that thought, but then he leaned forward again, capturing her lips in another searing kiss. This time it was softer, sweeter, and Hanna lost herself in it. His lips were tender against hers, teeth grazing her bottom lip, making her hips jerk towards him in desire. She wanted more and he gave it to her, tongue seeking hers, tasting and exploring the depths of her mouth.

Hanna's whole body was alight with pleasure, desire flooding her senses and scattering all rational thought. If Jori lifted his finger, if he said one word, she would have let him take her right there, consequences be damned. Every nerve ending in her body sparked and hummed with need.

And then he was pulling away, his lips soft and swollen from their kiss.

Hanna reached up and touched her own lips, the move too revealing, even though she couldn't stop herself. The kiss was too much. She was sure every emotion, all of the lust and confusion, and even a startling hint of like was showing on her face. She couldn't look at Jori, couldn't see if he was reading it all.

There was something between them. It had flared to life that first day he walked into the interview room. It grew with every second they spent together.

And it terrified Hanna in a way the war never could. Who was this man to her? Why did he make her feel these things?

How could she make it stop?

She had no idea. And that scared her more than anything else.

But she could lock it down. For a minute. An hour. A day. For long enough to do the job.

She blew out a breath and refused to think about how she could still taste Jori on her lips. "Come on. I'll show you those tricks I was telling you about."

If she didn't mention this kiss, maybe they could pretend it had never happened. Or that it was some kind of mistake.

But if *that* was a mistake, she never wanted to do anything right again.

Jori saw Hanna working behind the bar of The Docking Station but forced himself not to stare. He offered the short brunette beside her a smile and sauntered up, ordering his drink before finding a table that put him close enough to where Morn Kark held court but didn't make it look like he was trying to ingratiate himself.

The Docking Station was an old relic of a bar, the name a throwback to when this area had been home to a spaceport dock that launched goods up to ships orbiting the moon. There were a few hints to that history in the décor, including a large painting of a Zulir with wings spread wide, floating in the vast darkness of space. But mostly the place was dark and a little rundown. The floor was sticky in a way no mop could clean up, and everything smelled faintly of liquor.

The picture in his file made Kark look like a bruiser. In person, the truth was clear: he didn't just bruise, he broke bones.

Half a dozen men sat around him, some trying to squeeze in but stuck behind more favored members of the gang. At Kark's right was Rexx, his second in command. Jori also recognized Jursor Hansyn. He didn't have names for the others, not yet.

But this was only day one.

The cute brunette came out balancing a tray precariously on one hand. She set the beers down in front of the gang before Kark grabbed her waist and pulled her down to his lap, smothering her in a passionate kiss.

That would make her Zilly.

No one batted an eye when the boss slid his hand up Zilly's skirt and made her moan. There were plenty of dark corners in the bar, and though no one had crossed any lines of decency yet, it was early. This was a wild bar. Jori expected he might learn a thing or two about public sex before this was all done.

Kark let Zilly go after another minute and all the men grinned after her, but no one dared to touch.

Jori wasn't subtle about watching the interplay.

He wanted Kark to notice him, he needed an in with the gang. But this wasn't the kind of place where he could fill out an application. When Hanna walked in to interview for the bartender gig, Zilly had thrown an apron on her and told her to get working. They paid in cash, and taxes were an afterthought.

If nothing else, Ozar could get Kark for that.

Jori let his gaze drift back to the bar. Hanna was laughing at something Zilly said as if they'd been friends for years. When someone ordered a drink, she prepared it with quick hands and handed it over.

She looked like she belonged, and it made Jori's stomach twist in a knot.

It was beyond stupid. She was doing exactly what she was supposed to be doing. It was what he was supposed to be doing, too.

But if she could lie so easily here, was anything about her real?

What about the kiss?

Punt. Jori wasn't thinking about that. They hadn't said a word about it in the two days since it had happened, and he could take the hint. It was a mistake. Whatever their cover for the job, at home they were strictly professional.

But now that he'd had a taste of her, he was starving for more.

One of the men from Kark's table got up and pulled out the chair opposite Jori without asking. He slid into the seat and grinned. "Haven't seen you before."

Jori sipped his drink. "I'm new to the area."

"What's that jacket about?" Jori heard movement behind himself and saw a shadow before his shoulder was soaked with strong beer.

"Whoops!" laughed another of Kark's men.

Jori shrugged out of the jacket and laid it on the table, watching as the Synnr military insignia soaked up more alcohol. "No loss there." He didn't have to choke on the words. He was a loyal soldier, he believed in protecting his people. But the patch was just a patch. And he had a part to play.

The man who'd poured beer on him took another seat. This one was Jursor. He kept his dark, thinning hair short and wore an oversized leather jacket, as if that might make it look like he had bulk. Even sitting, he was tall, but Jori wasn't intimidated by tall men. He'd had an entire life preparing him for that. "I wouldn't wear that shit here," Jursor warned. "You wouldn't want to get it... dirty." He laughed again.

That braying laugh was going to get on Jori's nerves, and he decided that he was going to like destroying this man. He had to get at least some satisfaction from the job.

"It's the only coat I've got," Jori said simply. "Not like they pay us grunts enough to get by." That was a lie. Jori got paid plenty. It was a matter of practicality. Soldiers with debts were soldiers who could be bought, just like Kark's men were going to find out.

The first man spat on Jori's coat as if he expected him to flinch. "We don't need soldier boys here."

"I'm just having a drink." Jori kept hold of his beer. He didn't want them spitting in *that*. "And if it weren't for this stupid as *braz* war, I wouldn't even be a soldier anymore. But the higher ups aren't discharging anyone, no matter what our contracts say." He glared down at his jacket, but didn't spit.

"That so?" Now Jursor was sitting back in his chair and Jori reassessed the situation. He'd expected the first man to be leading this encounter, but Jursor was the one in charge. He was higher up in the gang. He'd be the one reporting back to Kark.

"I don't want to die for a bogus—" he cut himself off and took a long sip of his beer. Let them fill the rest in their minds. A bogus war? Queen? Kingdom? These were Apsyn sympathizers, but he had to be careful about how hard he sold his part. Blatant sedition would be a step too far.

Jursor and his friend let that sit. "So what brought you in here?" he asked. He kicked his feet up onto the table.

The treads of his boots were clean. Almost shiny. Either Jursor was surprisingly fastidious, or those boots were brand new.

"I live in the neighborhood and I've been admiring the bikes out front for the last few days. Then my girl," he nodded his head towards the bar, but didn't try to look for Hanna, "started slinging drinks here. Thought I'd check the place out."

Jursor pursed his lips. "Hanna's your girl? She sounds like an Apsyn."

When she spoke to Jori, her accent was as flat as any Synnr's, but she was playing up her lilting drawl for the crowd.

"What's that to you?" He put a bit of defensiveness in his voice and hunched his shoulders. "At least she's Zulir."

"And a very fine Zulir at that." Jursor's friend grinned lasciviously.

Jori lunged forward and grabbed the man's lapel, the zipper digging into his palm. "What's that supposed to mean?"

He held up his hands. "Nothing to it. Just appreciating someone from the old country."

Jori let him go. Jursor clamped him on the shoulder. "Enjoy your drink, soldier." He nodded to his friend and they left him alone.

First contact made. Jori watched them as they took their seats at Kark's table. Jursor's was still empty, but the other guy had to eject one of the hangers-on from where he'd been sitting. Jori thought he recognized the guy from the research file. Wrake. Or possibly Malo. The young man slunk up toward the bar with slumped shoulders, his moment passed.

Jori didn't look for Hanna. She was playing her part and he wouldn't overdo it.

But he was already ready for this job to be over.

―――

Slinging hard liquor to drunk bikers was easy, so long as Hanna remembered to jerk her hips out of the way before they could grab her ass.

Few people wanted anything fancy, and the one time some kid slumming it from the university had come in and tried to order something with more than three ingredients, Zilly had kicked him out on principle.

Zilly didn't fit. Hanna had names for all of Kark's gang, and she'd even shared a few words with the man himself. He was a brute and about three seconds away from laying Zilly out on his table and taking her in front of all his men, just to prove his masculinity.

Hanna figured the sexuality of the place should have bothered her more. Each night she'd worked, she'd caught more than one couple fucking in the back hall. And those were the discreet ones. On her last round of the bar, she'd caught a man on his knees between his girl's thighs while she bit her lip to keep from making a sound. A man beside them had his hand on his cock.

If this place weren't home to a gang who bombed innocent people, she might have found it kind of hot.

An interesting thing to learn about herself, and an inconvenient place. But she could explore the fun of watching or being watched when she wasn't three wrong moves away from death.

"We're getting low on the whiskey," Zilly warned as she carefully placed an empty bottle in the discard bin.

"I thought I saw a few bottles in that cupboard." Hanna was busy cleaning glasses, but she had to keep basic inventory in her head. She might have been in the bar under false pretenses, but the bartender gig was legit.

Zilly rolled her eyes. "That's Morn's special stash.

He had it imported from—" she cleared her throat. "Anyway, it's all expensive and only for his guys. Not sure why he has to fill up my space when he has a nice big office to store it."

"Men have never been known for their logic." It was the right thing to say, even if Hanna had never quite understood those kinds of things. But she needed to bond with Zilly, and playfully complaining about their men was a sure way in. It was true on Kilrym and on Aorsa, and Hanna would be willing to bet it remained true on any planet where people formed romantic bonds.

Zilly opened a new bottle of whiskey and poured two shots, sliding one to Hanna. "You are a wise woman," she said as she downed hers.

Hanna toasted and drank, turning away as she did so and deftly dumping three quarters of the whiskey down the drain. She couldn't let her senses get dulled, and right now that was her biggest risk. Zilly poured free drinks like it was going out of style, though the alcohol never seemed to make her stumble. She just went and sat on Kark's lap for longer and longer, until she was flushed. Then she'd pull him into the back hallway and leave Hanna to handle the bar alone until she came back, hair mussed and with a big smile on her face.

Zilly didn't look like the kind of woman who belonged in a bar like The Docking Station. With a pang, Hanna realized why. Zilly reminded her of Luci. It wasn't in looks. Zilly had dark hair while Luci was blonde. Zilly was Zulir, Luci human. But they were both small and young and had an irresistible air of innocence to them. Even if it was clear that Zilly's innocence was... well, she definitely liked sex. As for naivety, Hanna wondered just how much she'd be stealing from this young woman before the job was over.

"Take these over to that table by the window, will you?" Zilly slid a tray of drinks Hanna's way.

Hanna picked it up and balanced carefully. If she was going to spill a drink on someone, it would be on purpose. And spilling a loaded tray of merchandise was likely to get her fired.

Three guys in rough clothes with rougher expressions sat at the table by the window. They didn't glance at Kark's table except for when his guys got loud. These weren't members of the gang, just locals who liked to drink.

"You're new, baby," said the first guy as Hanna started dishing out drinks.

"They're really upping the decoration," said the second.

The third slid a hand around her waist and Hanna had to stop herself from breaking fingers. She twirled around his hold with a laugh she hoped didn't sound forced and took a step back. "Enjoy the drinks, boys." Then she escaped before they could make any requests.

She could feel Jori's eyes on her as she sauntered back to the bar as if she didn't have a care in the world.

She risked flashing him a warning look. He couldn't be her savior. Yes, they wanted Kark to know they were an item, but she had to establish herself here on her own two feet.

Jori gave her a smile and pushed himself to his feet. What was he doing?

By the time she got back behind the bar, customers were lined up and Zilly was filling drinks as fast as she could. Hanna joined her and they had the line under control quickly.

"Nice work with those guys," Zilly said.

"Did you know they were handsy?" Hanna handed a pair of drinks to two waiting customers.

"One of them might have made a move the last time I walked by." Her eyes widened with worry. "Don't tell Morn, okay? If he intervened every time a guy got a bit grabby, we'd lose half our customers."

"You shouldn't have to put up with that." Hanna wondered if this was Zilly's naivety or something else.

The girl rolled her eyes. "No shit. But this bar has a reputation. If you're going to work here..." She let it trail off, and Hanna had to draw her own conclusions.

"Can I get another one please?" Jori asked. He finally made it to the front of the line. "How are you doing?"

Zilly stepped toward him, but Hanna cut her off. "I'm okay if this one gets a bit gropey." She leaned across the bar and kissed him on the cheek.

It's just for work, she reminded herself, even as his scent washed over her.

She heard Zilly's laugh distantly as she pulled away and poured a drink for Jori, whiskey for color, but mostly water.

"You should come sit with me and my guys," a man was saying to Zilly as she took his order.

"We're a bit busy here, sweetheart." She tried to take a step back, but he reached out and clamped a hand on her arm.

"Come on, we'll show you a good time."

Zilly struggled.

Before Hanna could step in, Jori tapped the man on the shoulder. And when the man glanced back at him, Jori leveled him with a punch.

The hush that fell over the bar was almost supernatural. Hanna didn't dare look over at Kark, but she hoped he was watching this.

Jori punched him again, this time in the stomach, and the man went down. Jori kicked him the rest of the way over.

"Are you okay?" he asked Zilly, speaking loud enough to project across the bar.

Zilly nodded, rubbing her fingers over her wrist.

Hanna heard a commotion and finally looked toward Kark. He was making his way towards them.

Once there, he clamped a hand on Jori's shoulder and grinned at Zilly. "Get this man a drink, girl! And someone get this piece of *braz* out of here!"

Hanna didn't smile at Jori, but it was a close thing.

They were in.

8

JORI HAD BEEN TRAINED to withstand torture. He knew the techniques. He could disassociate and offer no actionable information.

But if he was stuck here for much longer, he might break.

Or Hanna might realize just how much she affected him.

The bar was empty of everyone except for Kark's crew. It wasn't technically closed yet, but word seemed to have gone out that business was done for the night.

And Jori was sitting at his table with Hanna on his lap, her arm around his shoulders, and her upper body flush against his.

They needed to do this for the job. Kark was happy

with him for that act of chivalry with Zilly, and Hanna got to tag along as his woman. Even better, Hanna had warmed Zilly up so much that they kept trading banter.

If they could keep this up, the job might be done in a matter of days, rather than the weeks or months they had to be prepared for.

"So I was in the lead," Hanna started, regaling the group with a story from her childhood. "This bike was a piece of *braz*, I had to borrow it since my parents wouldn't get me one until I proved I really wanted to race. I was maybe a kilometer or two from the finish line, and the damn thing stalls out."

There was an uproar at the table and Hanna nodded, encouraging it.

How was she nodding with her whole body?

And how could his be on fire with lust in the middle of a mission?

"Did you get it fixed?" Zilly asked. She was perched on Kark's knee, rather than completely pressed against him.

"I didn't know how!" Hanna's voice had taken on a tone Jori didn't recognize. She was bright and animated and completely open, telling her life story to her brand new friends.

Was it even her life story?

He pushed the thought aside. Doubting her now would put the mission in danger. He had to believe every word she spoke like she was a priestess in the temple on a holy day.

Though if he were going to worship her, it would be far more sensual than a normal prayer.

"The first bike passed me while I was trying to get it restarted. Then the next. I tried to flag down help, but we were in the middle of the race and no one was going to stop to help me. Once I figured out I couldn't fix it, I grabbed onto the front wheel and started dragging it. Unsurprisingly, I finished last. But my parents bought me my first bike after that. It was this used SynStar that was battered all to *braz* but ran like a dream."

"Your first bike was a SynStar?" Kark asked. He'd been laughing along with the rest of them as Hanna told her story, but this was the first thing he'd asked her.

She nodded. "My dad knew a guy who knew a guy, and so on. When I was older I got to tour the factory once. It's amazing."

"This is why we need to visit the homeland." Kark pulled Zilly back and kissed her neck. "Nothing like that up here. There's real history down on Kilrym. If it weren't for this useless war..." Kark stared at Jori, silently daring him to say something.

Jori sipped his drink. He had to be careful about that. Even with the watered drinks Hanna had been slipping him, he could feel the buzz in the back of his head. And now he was drinking from the same bottle as the rest of the gang. He couldn't let himself go overboard.

"Ugh!" Zilly groaned. "Enough about the home country, love. I'm sure Hanna doesn't want to talk about it."

"I don't mind, really," Hanna said. She reached for Jori's drink and took her own sip. "It's nice. Jori's been great, letting me tell him all my boring old stories. But with the war, a lot of people don't want to hear it. As if I'm going to... I don't even know. Like I'm some sort of Apsyn spy or something."

He was going to kill her.

But Kark laughed, and after a moment Zilly giggled. The rest of the crew joined in.

"As if we're not all really Apsyns," Kark finally said. "No such—mmph!"

Zilly kissed him hard and Kark clamped a hand on her head, holding him close. When he let her go, they were both a bit breathless. "Dance with me," she commanded.

He yelled a command to the speaker system and the music changed, then he turned to his men. "See if those girls on the corner are still out there and invite them in. You all need dance partners. And they could use some coin."

Jori tightened his hold on Hanna, as if one of the men might dare to reach for her or she couldn't defend herself.

"Time to make our exit?" he whispered against her neck.

She leaned into him with a soft smile. "I think we have to dance. It's going well. Play it up."

Kark and Zilly were grinding together to the sensual music, and a few minutes later, Jursor led three women inside who were surrounded by the other members of the gang.

They wouldn't just be dancing for long.

"We slip out when it gets wild," Hanna told him as she slid off his lap and grabbed his hand, pulling him out of his chair. "Once someone is sucking Kark, he'll forget all about us."

Already it seemed like the gang had forgotten they were there. But Zilly did smile over at Hanna when she and Jori started dancing next to her and Kark.

Jori's spine was stiff. Every sway of his movement was wooden, and he probably looked like a schoolboy dancing with a girl for the first time. Hanna was liquid around him, her body clinging to his and guiding him as if it was her only task in life.

Jori tried to focus on the movements, to loosen his body and sway with her, but her curves pressed against him wove a seductive spell that he couldn't ignore. Every place they touched seemed alive, like an electric current bound them together.

He loosened up. There was no other option. Hanna was heat and sex and everything he couldn't want. And she was looking at him like he was her whole world.

He had to remember it was fake. This was for a job. All jokes aside, she was an Apsyn spy. Or rather, an Apsyn spying for the Synnrs.

Nothing between them was real. It couldn't be. The only thing that existed was the job.

When it finally happened, the kiss didn't feel pretend. The warmth, the spark firing in his blood, the way his heart raced in anticipation. He'd kissed before, too many times to count. He knew his reputation. No one permanent. Nothing beyond a night or two.

This kiss threatened to destroy his life.

That didn't stop him from deepening it with slow, sensual strokes of his tongue. The heat between them surged, and she moaned against him, letting him swallow the sound.

They were one swaying body of desire, and as his hand roamed down her side, she shivered. Jori wanted to roar in triumph. Her body didn't lie, and it was as much under this spell as he was.

He wanted this moment to last forever. This was a stolen fragment of what could have been, if they were different people.

But nothing could make their pasts evaporate, and Jori forced himself to pull back before he crossed a line he couldn't uncross.

Hanna stared up at him, and at some point she'd summoned her wings. They wrapped around him, hovering and hugging and hiding them from view of the rest of the crowd.

She wasn't the only one shining. Kark's red wings were flared wide as Zilly went to her knees in front of him and displayed her own lilac wings, using them to obscure her from view as she took him in her mouth.

One of the women from outside was wearing only her wings as two of Kark's gang kissed their way up her body, her head thrown back in pleasure.

And Jori had worried the kiss was risqué.

Hanna vanished her wings and nodded towards the door, holding her hand out to him.

No one noticed as they left.

Jori didn't drop her hand on the entire walk home.

————

Hanna heaved a crate off the pallet and carefully set it on the bar, grabbing two bottles of liquor and putting them in their place. Zilly had a whole stack of dirty glasses she was washing carefully, drying them off afterwards so thoroughly that not even a speck of water was left.

"It's just not the same," Zilly said, grabbing the next glass. "I don't know what it is, but something's different. Morn never used to be like this." There was a bit of a whine to her voice, but she was meticulously careful not to chip the cups.

Hanna hoped she sounded sympathetic. In the three days since Jori had gotten his in with the gang, Zilly had been complaining nonstop. And her complaints were frustratingly vague. "I'm sorry," she said. "Maybe he's just got something on his mind. You know how men are."

Zilly snorted. She stopped drying her glass and watched as Hanna heaved a second crate. "I don't think he even notices me outside of sex," she said. "We haven't had a decent conversation in weeks. And we were going to sneak over to our little hideaway, but he cancelled that!"

Morn Kark didn't seem like the kind of man to have heart to hearts with women, especially not with the girlfriend who was half his age. If Zilly was really Hanna's friend, she'd be giving her real talk. Hanna tried not to hate herself for her job. "Maybe he's just busy," she said. "The bar has been packed these last few days. And I know you've been having sex." She'd seen far more than she expected or wanted to.

Zilly's eyes went soft, and she smiled on a sigh. "Yeah, he never lets me down there. His tongue..."

"I'm sure." Hanna didn't need commentary. There was nothing attractive to her about Morn Kark, but she'd been living out a nightmare of sexual frustration, being so close to Jori. She didn't need to hear a well-fucked woman wax poetic about her man.

Especially not when that man was killing innocent people.

"What about you? You and the new guy disappeared early the other night." She gave Hanna a sly look.

"He's a bit shy." Hanna grinned as lewdly as she could. "But when we got home..."

"Don't keep him all to yourself. I expect you both to stay until the end the next time we party, even if you stick to one another." She picked up her next glass and started cleaning again. "Do you need help with those crates?"

"No, I think I'm good." Hanna rested for a moment and looked out at the room beyond the bar.

Only about half of Kark's usual crew were there. Kark, at his place of honor, Jursor beside him, Rexx on the other side, along with Maisam and Mardoz. They were drinking beer and laughing amongst themselves. It was early yet, but Hanna wondered where the rest of the crew was. And she wondered if Zilly's relationship troubles might have something to do with it.

If Kark had a big job coming up, maybe he wouldn't pay so much attention to his girl.

Jori walked in and was greeted like a conquering hero. Once he'd been invited to Kark's table, the guys had accepted him as one of their own. It got even better when he brought his bike around. She'd given him enough information to speak with the passion of the newly converted, and he could rattle off enough fusion bike facts to bore the rest of the gang. He'd even gone with them on a ride the other day while Hanna and Zilly cleaned the bar.

But they hadn't shared any secrets. Neither had Zilly.

The smart play would be to wait it out. To build

trust and hope that something eventually slipped. But urgency nagged at Hanna. She could feel in her bones that something was about to go down, and she and Jori had to find out what and put a stop to it.

It wasn't just her own self-preservation talking, though that was a part of it. If they failed to act quickly and people died, Hanna suspected the blame would fall on her just as hard as it fell on Morn Kark. This was her chance to prove herself and gain her freedom. She couldn't fail.

She rolled her head from side to side, stretching her neck and catching Jori's eye in the process. Then she rolled her head towards the hallway and lifted an eyebrow. He gave his head a minute shake, but she flashed a look that said she was doing it.

A bit of telepathy, or some kind of comms device would have gone a long way. She needed Jori to keep the guys distracted. But they'd planned for this possibility. Kark and his men were busy and thin on the ground. The bar wasn't that packed, and Hanna had a good excuse to head out back.

"I'm going to go swap out these crates. You good for a bit?" she asked Zilly, knocking her hand against the wooden crate.

"Better you than me. My arms ache just thinking about it!"

Hanna loaded her stack of crates onto the dolly and carefully rolled it through the bar. She had maybe five minutes before someone noticed she was gone and another five before someone came to look. Plenty of time.

She shoved the crates into the storage room. Hanna took a deep breath to get herself in the right headspace. She'd done more dangerous jobs than this, and she'd never had backup before.

It would be fine.

Kark's office was two doors down from the storage room. The other doors were smaller storage closets and one unused office. The final door in the hallway led to a closet that held a massive safe. Hanna didn't have the time or the tools to pick the lock, so she left that for later. Maybe Jori would have an idea.

The office wasn't particularly neat. Kark had papers scattered all over his desk, and the whole place smelled vaguely like whiskey and cigar smoke. There was a computer screen on the desk, but it was powered down. Hanna tried to turn it on, but it had a biometric lock.

Good security, but not outside the norm. If he had regular financial data on that computer, the lock made sense. It didn't need to be hiding anything criminal.

She did know how to get around it, but it would

take time and she'd need to come back with a digital lock cracker to do it.

If she did this right, it wouldn't be her only chance.

Hanna sifted through the papers, careful to keep them spread out across the desk, just as Kark had left them. There were invoices, brochures for liquor and bike parts, and message slips in Zilly's handwriting. Nothing damning. But Kark was smart enough not to leave incriminating documents out in the open like that, especially not in an unlocked office.

If Hanna was a dastardly spy, she wouldn't leave anything in her official office. It was too obvious. But it was also something she couldn't ignore.

She pulled open the drawers of the desk. There was a tourist guidebook of Vanen, the capital of Kilrym. And there was a smaller map of Osais.

Hanna carefully removed it from the drawer and spread it out on the table. There were no markings, nothing conveniently circled with a label of "next bombing target," but she didn't let that discourage her.

She took a picture of the map with her communicator before taking a better look. It was a map of the same quadrant of the city where the first bomb had hit. The paper's fold creased along the same street that had been targeted, but that could be a coincidence.

The map had to be hiding some kind of secret. Hanna was tempted to stuff it in her pocket and take it with her, but if Kark noticed it missing, that could ruin everything.

She folded it back up and put it in the drawer before checking the time.

Her ten minutes were up. Every second she stalled now was begging for discovery.

Hanna slipped out of the office and was closing the door behind her when Rexx, one of Kark's men, barreled her way, demanding, "What were you doing in there?"

9

HANNA DIDN'T FREEZE. Freezing would get her killed. She lifted her hand from the doorknob and let it drop, giving Rexx her brightest smile and hoping it worked.

"I'm getting some fresh booze for the bar. Is there a problem?" She didn't let her expression slip and kept her breathing even.

You did nothing wrong, she told herself. *You're completely innocent.*

Lying to herself was the key to lying to other people.

Rexx jerked his thumb towards the storage room. "Whiskey's in there. Boss's office is off limits."

Hanna put her hand back on the knob and opened the door, taking a look inside. "*Punt!* I got turned around. We should really label the doors back here."

"Close the *punting* door right now," Rexx demanded. His jaw firmed, and Hanna felt a crackle of electricity in the air as he summoned his spark.

Hanna slammed the door and took a step back. "I'm sorry! It was an accident! Please, I need to get back and help Zilly. I'm sure it's getting busy."

Rexx took a step closer and flared out his wings. They were bright green with streaks of yellow in them. He didn't deserve the vibrant color.

Reflexively, Hanna flared out her own wings and spread them wide. If he was going to try and fry her with his spark, she'd hit him back twice as hard.

"Oh, you silly girl." Rexx smiled a predator's grin, sharp teeth showing. Some people described Zulir canines as fangs, and his were sharp enough to prove them right. "I think you were snooping. The boss won't like that."

Hanna's wings drooped. "You don't have to tell him."

You did nothing wrong.

You're completely innocent.

And you're afraid.

Rexx sauntered closer, his spark strong enough to make her hair stand on end, even though all he'd done was summon his wings. He was nearly as strong as a

Matched Zulir all on his own. Maybe she really should be afraid.

"And what will you give me to keep my mouth shut?" He reached out and swiped his thumb over her lips.

Hanna had to suppress the urge to bite him. "I have a boyfriend." She really didn't want to get on her knees for this guy.

"Demons love to share." Rexx moved to touch her shoulder, his palm trying to press her down.

Hanna resisted. "What's a demon?" She had her briefing, but no one had uttered the fusion cycle club's name to her in the bar. Hanna the innocent bartender had no idea.

Rexx pressed harder. "I'll show you."

"What's going on back here? Babe?" Jori's broke washed over her, and Hanna let out a breath. Then she tensed up even more.

She could handle Rexx. She wasn't going to suck his cock, but in another minute she could have talked him around.

Jori complicated things.

She was still glad he was there.

She glared at Rexx and he took a step back, lifting his hand from her shoulder. "Your girl here was sneaking around. What's that about, soldier boy?"

Jori looked from Hanna, to the door, then to Rexx. Then he grinned, and it was strange on his face. He never looked so carefree.

Maybe that only happened when he was on the job.

"Babe, I said to meet in the empty office. Next to Morn's." He grinned at Rexx. "I'd stuff her face in front of everyone, but my girl is shy."

Hanna glared. "That's private, *babe*." And they were going to have to get their stories straight. He was supposed to be the shy one. At this rate, they were going to have to participate in an orgy just to prove their loyalty.

Well. There were worse loyalty tests.

"I saw her coming out of Kark's office," Rexx pressed. "She can't be in there."

"I wasn't coming out of it!" she lied. "I was going into it because I thought it was where I was supposed to meet Jori."

"I thought you were getting more supplies for the bar."

Henchman shouldn't have decent memories. It made her job so much harder. "That was a lie," she admitted. "I didn't want to get Jori in trouble. He likes—"

"Babe," Jori cut her off, as if he expected her to describe some sort of unspeakable sexual act.

Rexx laughed. "With a mouth like hers, there's more than enough to share." He looked over at Jori, as if Hanna's opinion didn't matter.

Before this job was over, she was going to do a world of hurt to Rexx. No. A *galaxy* of hurt.

"I'm not the sharing type," Jori said. There was no trace of a grin this time. He looked past Rexx and met her gaze head on. His words held the weight of truth.

This job didn't have any room for the truth.

"You should probably head back, Han, it's getting busy out there. We can... you know... later." He stepped in close to Rexx and grabbed her hand, pulling her away from Kark's door and out of Rexx's reach.

"I'm not done here," said Rexx.

"Bring it up with Morn." He pulled her a few steps, and Hanna went willingly. She was almost ready to breathe a sigh of relief, or would have, if Jori wasn't holding on so tight.

He'd have a lecture for her when they got home, she was sure of it. He hadn't wanted her to take the chance. But if they got out of this hallway unscathed, she'd know she was right. Tiptoeing around would never get the job done. They had to take risks.

"Bring what up with Morn?" Kark said, turning the corner and blocking off their escape.

"Boss—" Rexx tried to say something, but Kark held up a hand to silence him.

Hanna jumped to speak before Jori could. She had a feeling he would try and protect her virtue or something inanely chivalrous like that. Chivalry had no place in spy work.

"I snuck back here to take care of my guy." She smacked her lips together and grinned, pulling out of Jori's hold and slinging her arm around his shoulder. "We just had a little bit of a mix-up. Now it's too late and I gotta go help Zilly before it gets too busy." She heaved a sigh. "Later, babe." She kissed his cheek. "I promise I'll do that thing you like when we get home."

Jori sucked in a ragged breath, and Hanna tried to ignore the things that did to her body. This was supposed to be a ploy, she wasn't supposed to actually get turned on by the thought of a quickie with her fake boyfriend.

But Jori had that effect on her no matter what.

"Zilly has the bar under control," Kark said. He grinned over at Rexx. "You wanted to see what this girl's got?"

"New guy said he doesn't share." Rexx glared.

Kark raised his eyebrows at Jori, who just shrugged.

"She's that good? Let's see it." He nodded toward Hanna to sink to her knees.

Jori tried to back up towards the empty closet. "A bit of privacy, man?"

Kark laughed and shook his head. "You say she's worth it, I want to see what all the fuss is about. I love my girl to death, but even she knows when it's time to share."

Hanna was ready to get this over with, but Jori shifted a bit so he was gripping the arm she had slung over his shoulder. She couldn't do as Kark commanded without struggling with him. And that would *not* sell this job.

"Can't say I like being watched, boss."

"She sucks your cock, or you both walk out of my bar and don't come back. Got it, soldier boy?" Kark scowled at Jori and neither man blinked.

Jori was a man who'd break before he bent. And Hanna wasn't just on this job because of her knowledge of bikes. She wasn't going to let him ruin this.

She leaned in close and whispered against his ear so only he could hear. "It's fine, Jori. Let me do this." She kissed his neck for good measure before pulling away. That was enough to break the staring contest with Kark, and he looked at her.

Jori looked like a man facing a firing squad, but only for a moment. Then he remembered they had an audience and grinned.

Hanna sank to her knees.

———

Jori could feel Kark's eyes on him. Rexx was there too, but he wasn't the threat. If they didn't do this, the mission was over.

But how could Hanna look at him again if he forced this on her?

She said it was okay, but he still wanted to slug Kark and make a run for it. They didn't deserve to see her like this.

That he could do something about.

Jori flared out his wings and did his best to engulf Hanna in them. He could feel a crackling energy where his wings hovered close to hers, and it only made his body light up more.

He worried for a moment he wouldn't get hard. This was not the ideal situation, no matter how skilled Hanna's tongue, but when she knelt at his feet and tilted her head up towards him, he was lost.

Hanna's eyes were a spark of light in the dark, and everything else fell away. His heartbeat kicked up, even as blood flooded low, making his cock heavy. It thickened, begging for her attention, and Jori didn't try and hold back.

Gently, he brushed away a strand of hair that had fallen across her forehead, tucking it behind her ear. Her skin was like silk under his fingers. Hanna closed her eyes and breathed deep.

Then she grinned, eyes still closed, and leaned forward, rubbing her cheek against the clothed cock in his pants.

Jori bit back a groan. If they were alone, he'd give her every noise. But he needed to steal as much privacy as he could.

Hanna ran her hands over his hips, the featherlight touch strong enough to brand him. It was the most charged moment of his life and he was still fully clothed.

But not for long.

With delicate fingers, she undid the fastening of his pants and freed his cock.

She didn't give him a chance to hesitate before licking a long stripe along his cock and then taking his head into her mouth. This time Jori couldn't stop the groan of pleasure, and he didn't care.

His hand hovered over Hanna's hair for just a moment before he clamped down, not quite holding her in place, but guiding her.

Not that she needed it.

Her tongue was a wicked instrument and Jori squirmed under her song. She sucked him deep, taking him to the back of her throat until he was sure she'd choke. Then, just before it was too much for both of them, she'd pull back.

He thought he heard a sound, but it didn't come from Hanna, so what did it matter?

Her tongue brought him close to the edge, pleasure building and building until he was sure he'd burst. It was too much to do anything but that. But Hanna seemed determined to savor it.

And, as much as it should have shamed Jori, he wanted that just as much. This might be the only time he had her like this. She might hate him once she stood, might tell him to go to *braz* and stay there for good.

He'd deserve it. Any man who could enjoy being forced into this situation deserved it.

And any man who could resist was a saint.

He needed to find his control and grasp it. If he dug his fingers into Hanna's hair and fucked her face, this would be over in a minute. Distantly, he knew that was what Kark would want to see.

But Kark had no place in this moment. Jori pulled his wings in tighter, heedless of the way they threatened to touch Hanna's.

It was a risk to get so close to another's wings. A Zulir's spark could fry another person with little effort. But Hanna wouldn't do that to him. If she ever planned violence against him, she'd get up close.

She couldn't get any closer now.

He surrendered to the heat of her tongue and mouth, finally curling his fingers into her hair and thrusting. His entire body was alive with need, all of it attuned to the woman on her knees in front of him.

She was everything. And no matter what anyone might think, she was the one in control of this moment.

Every nerve sang with bliss, and he couldn't stop now. His teeth clenched, trying to hold back. But Hanna showed him no mercy, and with a gasp he came, seed spilling.

Hanna leaned back, wiping her swollen mouth. Now she looked like some fallen angel, wings drooping and body made for sin.

He should have been sated. Instead he wanted to

lay her flat out and feast on her until she was crying out in pleasure.

Jori forced himself to calm down. Now was *not* the time. He rearranged his pants until he was something approaching decent, though he was sure his cheeks were flushed and pupils blown.

Hanna stood and gave him a nod. "I need to get back to work." She wiped some of the dust from her knees and left him alone.

And he was completely alone. Kark and Rexx were no longer in the hallway. When had they left?

Could he have pulled away from Hanna before...?

Jori forced the thought out of his mind. He took another minute to gather his thoughts before forcing himself to walk back into the main area of the bar, where Kark gave him a broad grin and slapped him on the back while Rexx summoned Zilly to bring Jori a drink.

To sell the job, Jori had to smile. He had to listen to the vulgar jokes from Kark's crew and laugh along. He couldn't look at Hanna. If he did that, he'd give it all away.

But he feared he'd crossed a line he couldn't uncross. He just had to wait for the consequences.

10

Hanna saw when Jori took off. He'd brought his bike to the bar, but they were supposed to ride home together.

Then Kark had to go and ruin it.

Hanna compartmentalized for the rest of the night. If she let herself remember the taste of Jori, the way his skin felt under her fingers, she'd be a mess of nerves and heat.

She had to fix this.

Jori hadn't looked at her for the rest of the night. They couldn't go on like that. She spent the rest of her shift dreaming up conversations they'd have to speak and wishing it could all be solved with a kiss.

And she was a bit... disturbed... by how much she'd liked it. Kark and Rexx weren't the audience she would have chosen, but knowing she was being watched, even through Jori's wings, had made it even hotter.

Yeah, Hanna definitely had to stop thinking about that.

In the small hours of the morning, she made it home. She expected Jori to be asleep. Or gone. If he couldn't face her at the bar, their tiny house would be so much worse.

She found him sitting on the couch, holding a decorative ball in his hands and tossing it from one hand to the other. He didn't glance at her when she walked in and locked the door.

The bedroom was calling to her for more than one reason. But it would be beyond easy to go to sleep and pretend that all would be well in the morning. She and Jori would have plenty of time to build their emotional walls back up, and they could play this off as just part of the job.

Hanna's job made her a liar, but she was trying not to lie to herself. She forced herself to cross the room and sat in the chair closest to Jori.

When he looked at her, there was dread in his eyes.

"Why are you looking at me like that?" It came out a bit defensive. But the compartmentalization that worked so well at the bar suffered a structural failure the second she spoke with Jori.

"If you need to report me for disciplinary action, I'll cooperate. My behavior was—"

"Don't finish that sentence." Hanna's mind whirled, trying to catch up with what he was saying. "Have you been spiraling all night?"

Jori jolted. "I wouldn't call it spiraling. I've been thinking."

"There's your problem." She ran her fingers through her hair and shook it out. "You saved my ass back there. Maybe I could have talked Rexx around, but I'd much rather suck your cock than his."

That startled a choked laugh out of Jori.

"We both knew this might happen," she continued. "Are you going to be okay?"

That got him to meet her gaze again. "I should be asking you that. How can I make it up to you?"

"Only one of us got off." Her words dropped like a bomb.

Hanna shouldn't have said it. It was one thing to suck him off when their cover depended on it. Otherwise they were supposed to keep things professional. But it had been a long day. She was stressed.

And she'd spent hours trying and failing not to think about how Jori could return the favor.

His breath turned rough. "That's true." He put the ball he'd been messing with aside and leaned forward.

Hanna needed to get up. She needed to step into a cold shower and pretend she hadn't said anything. Her fingers were more than adequate for relieving the tension. She didn't need Jori.

But her body craved him.

"We shouldn't," she managed to say, even as her body swayed closer to his.

He reached out and placed his hand on her thigh, his palm burning against her skin as he slowly slid it up to tease the hem of her skirt. "It's a bad idea," he agreed, letting his fingers flirt with her inner thigh.

Hanna let her legs fall open. "We're just making things even."

"Yeah," he breathed out as she surged forward and captured his lips.

Jori tasted of whiskey and something else smoky and sweet she couldn't place. His hands clamped onto her hips, holding her on his lap as he took control of the kiss and devoured her.

She wanted to be devoured.

Jori's cock was hard between them, a promise of what he could give her if only they could get out of all of their clothes. Need burned hot within her, smoldering right along with her spark.

She could practically feel electricity arc between them, but it was impossible, a flight of fancy brought on by pleasure and need.

Jori flipped them and Hanna held on, but he wouldn't let her tumble to the ground. Suddenly she was the one sitting on the couch while he went to his knees and looked up at her like a supplicant.

Had he felt this exposed in the hallway?

He slid his fingers up her legs and under her skirt, hooking onto her panties and pulling them down. Hanna felt stripped bare, even though she was mostly covered. But from where Jori was kneeling, he could see it all.

And the man was famished.

He kissed up her thighs, each a promise of pleasure that sent shivers down her spine. The anticipation was almost enough to make her moan with need.

When his tongue touched her pussy, Hanna's back arched and she didn't recognize the wanton noise that spilled past her lips. It was pure sensuality, a whole language that didn't need syllables.

And he was only getting started.

Hanna clutched at the couch cushions, biting her lip in pleasure as Jori explored further, delving into her with an expertise that terrified and thrilled in equal measure.

Jori licked and kissed like his life depended on it, teasing delicate circles around the tightly wound bundle of nerves between them before finally falling into an almost dizzying rhythm that sent tendrils of pleasure spiraling through Hanna's body in time with every stroke he made.

Hanna clung desperately onto whatever shreds remained from reality—but that reality was quickly dissolving under Jori's tongue. What did she care about the world when she had Jori between her thighs, bringing her to heights of pleasure she could barely imagine?

She could feel the tremors of orgasm building, threatening to overwhelm her. Hanna reached for control, for something that would keep her on this cliff's edge. She wasn't ready to tumble over just yet, not when it felt like they'd barely started.

She wanted all the pleasure he could give her, she greedily wanted to come and come until it was all she was. But if she came, it was done. And she couldn't let this end, not yet. She wasn't ready.

How was she supposed to get up and walk away like everything was normal between them?

Her fears and worries washed away as Jori's fingers joined his tongue, and then everything else fled too. She gasped out Jori's name as release wracked her body. The pleasure was so strong it almost hurt, but all she could do was beg for more.

Jori didn't stop. He kept up his tongue hot on her until the waves of pleasure ebbed into something calmer, something almost manageable. It wrecked her harder than the orgasm.

Her body was drunk on pleasure, and she barely knew what she was babbling out. "I think that makes things even," she murmured.

"No." Jori stood and leaned over her, his eyes still burning with desire. "I think it was a good start."

———

Stepping into the bedroom was crossing a line. But with the taste of Hanna still hot on his tongue, Jori left his cares behind. He and Hanna had raced across every line already, and there was no going back. Not tonight.

It was surreal that they were still fully clothed. His cock pressed against the closure of his pants and Hanna's cheeks were flushed.

Jori stepped close and his hands glided up Hanna's body, fingertips tracing the curve of her hips and up to the swell of her breasts. Her nipples were tight buds pressing through her shirt, and she sucked in a deep breath when he ran a thumb over one.

He wanted to explore every inch of her until he memorized every response. And then he wanted to perfect his touches until he had her quivering under him with just a brush of his fingers or a whispered word. Hanna soaked up the pleasure like she was made for it, eyes drifting closed as she swayed closer to him.

He was tempted to rip her shirt right down the middle and feast on what he revealed, but he held himself back, instead helping her pull it over her head and toss it aside. Her bra went next.

Punt. She was perfection.

Jori pulled her closer, no longer able to resist the temptation of her lips. She opened under him, tongue brushing against his. His hands continued their journey downwards, even as he devoted himself to the kiss. She was down to only her skirt now, with nothing beneath it.

He slid his finger under the clasp and held it there, waiting.

Hanna's breath hitched in anticipation, and then she kissed him deeper. She covered his hand with her own and helped him unclasp the skirt and let it fall to the floor.

All the while, his lips never left hers.

He eased her back towards the bed and followed

her down, groaning as one of her legs wrapped around him. Even with his pants still on, he could feel the heat of her. Her skin was everything he'd ever dreamed of and he wanted to lose himself in it.

His fingers flirted against the wet heat at the core of her, teasing her entrance before gliding inside. Hanna moaned and arched against him. Before he could do more, she pulled at his own shirt and he had to break the kiss for a moment to tear it over his head and fling it away somewhere.

"Take your *punting* pants off," Hanna demanded breathlessly between kisses.

Her wish was his command.

Every second away from her was too much, and when he came back to the bed, naked, cock hard and ready, he pressed his body fully against hers and captured her lips again.

He could kiss her forever.

His fingers dipped inside her again, pushing further until he found the spot that made her whole body go tight with a shock of pleasure as her breathing quickened. She didn't hold anything back from him and Jori gave her everything he could in return.

As much as he loved the kiss, Jori broke away with a groan and began to explore her body. His lips moved lower, and he took one nipple into his mouth and teased it with his tongue.

Hanna gasped, arching against him and pressing her breast even closer. Jori smiled against her skin and didn't relent, seducing her with his tongue until she cried out for more. He rolled onto his back, taking her with him so she straddled him.

They paused in that moment, gazes locked as something impossibly tender passed between them. It made Jori's heart thump and made him question everything he thought he knew about this woman. He couldn't let that show, couldn't give her that power over him, even as he feared he was putting his whole self in her hands.

He pulled her down into a scalding kiss.

Then his fingers were back at her entrance, teasing her clit until she bucked against him, his own cock tortured by the movement.

He slid two fingers inside of her, meeting the irresistible heat and tight wetness that he'd never forget.

And once she was stretched and ready, he replaced his fingers with his cock, thrusting into her in a single stroke.

Hanna gasped and dug her fingers into his shoulders hard enough to bruise. He'd gladly wear her mark and hope it never faded.

They moved together, the harmony as natural as it was sensual. She was tight and wet, and it took all his control not to spill right there. But he needed to see her take her pleasure again. He needed it more than his next breath.

He thrust into her and heard his name escape Hanna's lips on a desperate breath. He wanted to hear it again and moved faster, pushing her higher until she was clinging to him, out of control but still in perfect balance with him. She flung her head back and bit her lip, bouncing on him as they moved, but the only sounds that escaped were gasps and moans of pleasure that hit their crescendo and had her body rippling around him as she clung tight.

The pleasure was too much for Jori, but he tried to hold on, even as his cock began to vibrate with the inescapable need for completion. He wanted this to last forever, to revisit it in his dark days and know that he'd had this one perfect moment, where Hanna's face was contorted in pleasure, all walls gone as she surrendered and accepted what he gave her.

Then he let go, the release thundering through him so strongly that he bellowed in pleasure and his vision momentarily whited out.

When his heart beat started to calm, Hanna lay

down next to him, body pressed tight, and Jori flung an arm around her.

Doubts threatened to creep in, and they warred with the emotions roaring strong from so deep inside of himself that he didn't realize they were there.

From the moment they'd met, she'd made him feel something almost indescribably strong. Animosity. Loathing.

Desire.

The first two had burned away and all that was left was the desire. And in the embers of his emotions, he could feel other things growing. Tenderness. Hope.

He didn't have time for this. Jori was a loyal Synnr soldier. He had goals, plans. None of those included falling for a reformed Apsyn spy.

But all of that was far away. Hanna's breathing evened out and Jori stared at her. Light from outside filtered in around the corners of the curtains, just enough to make out her relaxed features.

He'd never had trouble leaving a bed when it was time to go. The smart move would be to slide out from under the covers, shower off the scent of her, and sleep on the couch where he belonged.

The couch that was indelibly imprinted with her memory.

Instead of walking away, Jori pulled Hanna closer

and pulled the sheets up around them. He was warm and content. Trouble would come for them later. They'd have to court it to get the job done. But tonight Jori could sleep and dream that when all of this was done, Hanna really would be his.

11

WORK. Right. The job.

Hanna's body ached in all the right places, and she'd found bruises on her hips in the shape of Jori's fingertips. There was a hickey on her neck and she couldn't stop smiling.

Work.

He was still asleep. Hanna had slid out of bed and been determined not to wake him. When he woke up, they'd have to deal with the night before. When he woke up, she'd have to admit it had been a mistake.

But he wasn't awake yet, and Hanna refused to have that conversation with herself.

Instead, she looked at the projection of the picture she'd taken of the map in Kark's office. Blown up to three times its normal size, it still didn't tell her anything.

"What's that?" Jori asked as he padded downstairs, bare feet silent against the carpet.

Hanna nearly jumped out of her skin, but she kept her expression cool. Work. This was work. "I found this map in Kark's office and took a picture. It feels important. It's the same neighborhood where the bomb went off, but I'm not seeing any special notations or anything."

Jori approached slowly, keeping more than an arm's length of distance between them as he studied the projection. He reached out and tilted it to get a better look. "That's weird."

"What?" She angled her head to try and see what he was looking at.

"The street names are misspelled." He expanded the image until she could see the writing at the intersection: PRYMROSE WAY and SICAMORE STREET.

"The bomb was planted in a building at that intersection." She stared at the projection until her eyes burned, then she grabbed a tablet and pulled up a map of that area. "This map confirms those spellings are wrong."

"Did you think I was wrong?" Jori asked. He didn't take the tablet when she offered it.

"No, but I wanted to confirm it. For all I know, there was some famous Synnr family named Prymrose with a Y and that was what the street was named for. I trust you." That hung between them for a moment before Hanna stepped back to put even more distance between them.

This was going to be torture.

Jori took a deep breath. "We should—"

"I need to get back into Kark's office." She spoke over him before he could start a conversation she didn't want to deal with.

"What? No!" The denial was immediate and absolute.

"I need in his office and in his safe," Hanna continued, as if Jori hadn't objected. "The map is suggestive, but hardly damning. This could have been a legitimate misprint."

"That's doubtful," he muttered.

"Of course it's doubtful." Energy thrummed in Hanna and she wanted to move, but Jori was right there. If she got close, she might do something crazy, like touch him. "We're here for a reason. We need to do the job."

"We got caught yesterday." His breath hitched and his eyes darkened.

Hanna had to look away. She could remember the

taste of him, the feel of him inside of her. It was an echo in her skin. But she couldn't react. Jori already didn't trust her. If he accused her of using sex to manipulate him, she didn't want to contemplate what she would do. Or how it would shatter her heart.

"We played it off," Jori continued, his voice rough. "But getting caught two days in a row will arouse suspicion we can't brush off."

"Yeah, you might have to fuck me up against the bar to prove we're just sneaking away for quickies." She regretted the words as soon as she said them. She'd been a spy for months and she'd been okay at it. She had the kind of training most people would dream of.

And here she was, running her mouth like a person who said the first thing that came to mind every time.

Jori turned away from the projection and finally looked at her. "We should talk about that."

"I think we covered things last night." Her spine was as stiff as stone, and Hanna had to fight the compulsion to summon her wings and wrap them tight around herself.

"We really didn't." His voice had gone soft, almost gentle.

Torturous.

"We were riding an emotional high," Hanna forced out. "We got a bit carried away. We're both adults. It happened. *Braz*, I've heard that you've gotten carried away with plenty of people. No reason to make a big deal about it." She couldn't think about the way he'd made her gasp his name, the way it had felt like he reached deep inside of her and grabbed hold of her heart.

It was just sex. It had to be.

"We can keep things professional from now on." If Hanna said it out loud, maybe it would somehow become true.

"And if Kark summons us to one of his parties? What do you propose then?" he asked, arms crossed and foot tapping.

An avalanche of want threatened to consume Hanna. The perfect excuse for more. She was tempted to voice a wicked proposal, to claim that she and Jori had to keep sleeping together to sell the job.

As if one night together hadn't already torn her to shreds.

"We'll do our job," Hanna said. "If I have to suck your cock again to keep either of us from getting blasted into oblivion, I'll do it. But even if we're at one of Kark's parties, I'm sure we can play along to a certain point. We don't have to cross any lines."

"Care to define those lines?" His eyebrows were raised in challenge.

"I need to get into Kark's office." What she really needed was to get this conversation back on track. "Maybe you're right and today is a bad idea, but it has to happen soon. Our handler is going to want information."

"Or I can take a run at the office," Jori offered.

Hanna's immediate instinct was to quash the proposal. She forced that thought aside and nodded. "If you get the opportunity. The chance could come to either of us. Can you crack the safe?"

He opened his mouth and then closed it with a shake of his head. "Not an area of my expertise."

"I only have one set of safe cracking tools with me, and I didn't think to bring them to work. I can stash them there. The liquor storage room isn't locked. I'll hide the tools on the shelf just inside the door. There's a small first aid kit, it'll be right next to that." She hated to let the tool out of her possession, but if either of them got the chance, they had to take it.

"And if someone finds it?" he asked.

"It looks like a communicator. I'll have to add you to the ID scanner, otherwise the thing won't work. You just need to press it beside the lock and engage the cracking code. It takes anywhere from a few seconds to two minutes."

"Is this normal spy gear?"

"What? Do you think I was some kind of jewel thief before?" She laughed, but Jori had a contemplative look on his face. "Seriously? I would be living in a mansion with a dozen servants if I had jewel thief money. Not... this."

Jori's expression went blank. "Program the device and show me how to use it. We hit our targets before the week is out."

———

Dread settled over Jori like a cloak when he arrived at the bar. Hanna was smiling with Zilly and slinging drinks as if she'd been working there for years instead of a week.

Only a few of Kark's crew were there. Kark and his closest men were gone, and Jori was glad of it. He knew he should be using the opportunity to gently pry into the history of the Demons. Underlings might give him information by accident.

Instead he nursed his beer and watched Hanna.

He knew he should call last night a mistake. A

lapse in judgement that could lead to critical mission failure. A catastrophe.

But the only thing he wanted now was to take her away from this place and keep her safe.

Hanna must have felt his eyes on her. She looked over at him and their gazes locked. He shivered with the need for her and forced himself to look away.

At least they had to pretend they were together. If they had to be strangers, the mission would crash and burn.

"You alright?" Maisum, one of the newer men in Kark's crew, asked. "Trouble with your girl?"

Jori could give some gruff answer. Or a lewd one. What he couldn't do was pour his troubles out to a man who might be a terrorist. But he couldn't bring himself to make a lewd joke about Hanna.

He said nothing, and Maisum took it as an invitation to talk.

"I had a thing with this guy not too long ago and it went sour, so I know the look." He nudged Jori's shoulder in misguided solidarity. "It started out great, right? Could not keep our hands off of each other. His Match didn't like it, but she wasn't his wife."

"He had a Match?" Jori wasn't supposed to get pulled into the story, but he couldn't help himself. He didn't know why he'd asked the question. While many Matched Zulir couples and groups fell into romantic relationships, plenty were purely platonic. Others fell in and out of romance or allowed multiple people into their relationships. There was no one way to be Matched.

"Yeah, her family owned this toy company and they both worked for it. I tried to get him to come hang out here instead. He was wasting his time at NovaTek."

That name meant something to Jori, but he couldn't quite place it. "What's this got to do with me and Hanna?"

"Don't let stupid stuff get in the way. Life's too short." Maisum slammed down the rest of his drink.

And that's when Jori remembered NovaTek. It was one of the buildings destroyed by the bomb. The bomb Kark and his men might have set.

"Why'd you want him here? Was he into bikes?" And was Maisum involved?

Maisum shook his head. "Not a bit. He was more into itty-bitty robotics, so small you could barely see them. He tried to explain the tech to me once, but I didn't get it until... well, I'm not the type to get it, you know. He lost an arm in that bomb."

Before Jori had to think of a response, Kark, Rexx,

and Jursor burst into the room, and Maisum got up to greet them.

Jori took a mental note of Maisum's story, and the information about the type of robotics being built at the toy company. That could be important.

Kark settled into his seat at the head of the table and the rest of the guys fanned out around him. Jori was shunted to the seat furthest from Kark and had to strain to listen to the little jokes Rexx kept interjecting with.

He needed to get in Kark's good graces, but he didn't regret his seat. Half of Rexx's jokes were indiscriminately offensive, and the other half didn't even have punch lines. Even Kark got annoyed and sent him to get another round of drinks after awhile.

Another hour passed, and the table was full to bursting. Kark and Jursor had their heads together and were talking low.

Kark looked up and glanced at Jori. "Hey, new guy, go dance with your girl."

"She's busy." The night had picked up, and Hanna and Zilly had been in non-stop motion behind the bar every time Jori risked a look.

"She's on break," Kark insisted. "Go keep her company."

Real talk was about to happen and Jori didn't get

to hear it.

"You got it, man." Jori couldn't argue any further. And just because he wasn't there, didn't mean he wouldn't hear every word, eventually. One of the buttons on his coat had a recorder built into it and he and Hanna could listen in when they got home.

The bar wasn't too busy when Jori approached and waited towards the side. When Hanna spotted him, she gave him a wide smile and a kiss on his cheek. "What's up?"

"You're on break." He wrapped a hand around her waist. "Let's dance."

"We're busy," Hanna protested, but she didn't try and pull out of his embrace. Zilly was right there and could hear every word.

"Kark said you're on break." Standing so close to her was a special kind of torture, but Jori soaked it up.

"I'm fine," Zilly insisted from behind Hanna. "Go have fun. And tell me all about it!" she added with a cackle.

Hanna buried her head against Jori's shoulder and groaned as he tugged her away.

"What's that about?" he asked. The dance floor wasn't too crowded, though a group of three people gyrated together to the pumping beat.

"Let's just say that Kark bought it." She held his

hand and did a spinning maneuver that had Jori bending his arm practically backwards.

Now was the perfect opportunity to tell her what Maisum had let slip, but Jori didn't. The music shifted to something slow and sensual, and he had no choice but to pull Hanna close, their bodies flush together.

"Think we have enough time to slip away?" she asked, breath blowing over his ear.

"Too risky."

"No one's even watching us."

But Jori wouldn't let her go. All of Kark's men were at the table. One poorly timed bathroom break and their cover would be blown.

"We'll have another opportunity," he promised.

Hanna tipped her head back and looked up at him with eyes so dark, that for a moment he let himself forget about the job. There was only her and the music and her teasing fingers as she traced a path up his chest. He tightened his grip on her, as if there was any chance she might try and get away.

The sensual beat of the song shifted to something even more sultry. Any thought of using this as an opportunity to talk about the job evaporated.

There was something in Hanna's expression that Jori feared was mirrored in his own. Something desperate and vulnerable, something that belonged locked away by the strongest emotional walls a person could build.

Something that could be torn down with a single kiss.

He didn't kiss her, though the urge to do it drove him hard. He couldn't kiss her. Not here, where it was all an act. When he kissed her, he didn't want her to question his motives, even if he wasn't entirely sure of them himself.

Hanna made him question everything. What was right. What was wrong. Could a person really change? And what could he really have if he looked outside the narrow life he'd planned for himself?

If the dance went on much longer, he might have said something. But the song came to an end, and Jori couldn't figure out the right words to say.

The spell was broken when Kark called his name.

"I'm being summoned," he said, as if Hanna couldn't hear.

"Good dance." She brushed her lips against his in a nearly chaste kiss that still left him reeling.

Kark had to call his name again before Jori could force himself to walk away.

When he was back at the table, Kark clamped a hand on his shoulder before he could sit down. "Come on, new guy. We've got a job for you."

12

RIDING with Kark's Demons was nothing like riding with Hanna. They roared through the streets, completely heedless of anyone in their way. Jori was thankful for his helmet, which hid his wince at a near miss with a person cleaning up a stall and Jursor, who yelled a stream of curses at the man long after they were out of hearing range.

Jori didn't know what this job was. Given Kark's reputation and rap sheet, it could be bad. And Jori had to play along. This was his in. Sure, they let him sit at the table. But if he proved himself tonight, they'd no longer banish him when they started to talk business.

And the sooner they fully accepted him, the sooner this thing would be over.

For some reason, a reason Jori was purposefully

not thinking of, he didn't want the acceptance. He wanted to stay entrenched here for weeks, months even. Stuck at the bar with Hanna at his side.

In his bed.

He forced his mind onto the ride. She was a distraction he couldn't afford. A woman he couldn't have. She wasn't in his bed. Any intimacy between them was a mistake or a ruse. He had to accept that. There was no other way.

Kark led them down a narrow alley from an even sadder street than the one that housed The Docking Station. Detritus was piled up against the buildings, and it must have been weeks or more since a street cleaning bot came through. Trash overfilled a dumpster at the back of the alley, and the rats didn't bother to scurry, despite the bikes.

Brave rats.

Or maybe they just recognized their own kind.

It smelled, but Jori could tune out the sour odor, even as it coated his tongue.

He spotted a small lightbulb outside a door with a sign mostly covered with years of grime. Fally's.

The door burst open and a skinny man in threadbare clothes stumbled out, hunched and swaying with too much drink. He didn't look at any of the Demons but managed to give them a wide berth as he lurched onto the main street and disappeared.

The guys took off their helmets and Jori followed suit, waiting to see what instruction Kark would give. Maisum glanced his way, head tilted so it wasn't obvious, so Jori ignored it.

This was a test. His every action and reaction was about to be judged. He couldn't *punt* this up, no matter what they asked.

Bile churned in his stomach, but he ignored it. He'd been a soldier for years. He'd done nasty things in the name of the Synnr queen. This was just one more thing to add to the list.

"Maisum, guard the door out here, no one gets in," Kark instructed as he slid off his bike. "Rexx, you've got the door inside. No one gets out. Wrake, Malo, I want you at the end of the alleyway. Just in case things get dicey."

"You got it, boss," said Rexx. Maisum acknowledged the assignment with a nod.

Wrake opened his mouth to say something, but Malo smacked him on the side and they slunk off to guard the mouth of the alley, shoulders slumped in the knowledge they were on boring duty.

Maisum posted himself beside the door while

Kark, Jursor, Rexx, Mardoz, and Jori headed inside. Rexx closed the door behind them and barred it.

The inside of the place was somehow worse than the outside. It was dark as the long nights on Aorsa, with only little yellow pots of light illuminating the seats at the bar and a few of the tables. The rest of the place was in dim shadow.

A terrible place to fight.

Then, one by one, wings appeared. One set, then another, then another, until Jori counted eight sets. It lit the place better, but he didn't like two to one odds.

Kark's crew let their wings out and Jori joined them. "Fally!" Kark yelled, paying no attention to the patrons. "Get your stinking self out here!"

An aura of anticipation fell over the bar. Jori could feel it in the air.

A figure stepped out from the backroom, tall and broad, but in the dim light that was all Jori could tell.

"I told you I'm not paying, Kark." His voice was low and garbled, as if someone had punched him in the throat more than once and knocked something out of place.

Kark flared his wings out wide. "Then you shouldn't have set up in my territory."

Fally let out a laughing breath that made his

shoulders jerk. "I was here long before you. I'm not paying."

Kark nodded to Jursor, who sent a shot of his spark at a stack of glasses behind the bar. They exploded, shards flying everywhere. One of the patrons at the bar jerked a wing in front of himself to stop from getting cut.

"You can leave right now and we'll call it even," said Fally. He was still half in shadow and the only person who hadn't summoned his wings.

Jori was getting a bad feeling about this. Fally should have been more worried about Kark. No one would come to back him up, especially not with Maisum on the door. And even though the Demons were outnumbered, the patrons of the bar didn't look like fighters.

Kark nodded again, and this time Jursor aimed for bottles of alcohol. When the bottles shattered, the liquor ignited in a ball of flame that luckily burned fast and burned out before it could catch on anything.

"I suppose it has to be that way." Fally stepped out of the doorway and flared his wings.

Jori bit back a curse.

Fally's wings were bright white with flecks of blue lightning. And they were twice the size of anyone else's.

He had a Match.

A Matched Synnr team was worth a dozen unmatched soldiers. Jori didn't know if it was the same for Matched civilians, but he feared he was about to find out. Though, since everyone else around him had normal sized wings, Fally's Match wasn't in the bar.

If Kark didn't know about the Match, he didn't let it show. He lashed out at Fally, their sparks dancing in the air between them.

And then it was chaos.

The patrons leapt from their chairs in a formation that would have impressed Major Ozar. Two came for him, while the others attacked Jursor and Mardoz. No one got in between Fally and Kark.

The first patron, a man with red wings tipped in yellow, managed to swipe at Jori and slice his arm with one of the broken glass shards.

Jori paid that back with a whip of his own spark that made the man scream and collapse.

The other kept his wings ready, the pose indicating he had at least a little self defense training.

But he was no match for a trained Synnr soldier.

The pain of the wound on his arm disappeared as he fell into the fight, parrying each burst of spark with a lash of his own.

An errant spark from another attacker sent him staggering, and Jori spun to face the second opponent, all while keeping his spark flying at the first guy. But there was no one there.

This wasn't a battle, it was a brawl. And Jori had to stop playing nice.

He swiped an empty beer glass from the closest table and chucked it at his opponent, who wasn't expecting anything but more of Jori's spark. That distraction was enough to make the man drop his guard.

And then he dropped to the ground, a wound on his hip still sizzling.

Jursor and Mardoz had taken care of most of the others, while Rexx kicked a man who was already in a pile on the floor by the door.

Fally had Kark cornered. Kark's wings completely circled him, guarding his body from any blast, but making it impossible to send out a blast of his own. His spark was starting to flicker, the beats of it growing longer after each of Fally's attacks.

Kark couldn't hold on for much longer. And once his spark failed, a single blow from Fally would kill him.

And Jori could let it happen.

One lucky strike from Fally, and the problem of

Morn Kark would disappear. Men like Kark died in places like this all the time. Kill the leader and his minions would scatter.

Making the job ten times harder.

Kark was a means to an end, and Jori had to see it through.

Fally was so focused on Kark, or so sure that no one would intervene, that he paid no attention to the rest of the fight. Jori took an open shot at his back, and Fally screamed in rage and turned the full force of his Matched fury focused directly on Jori.

Jori pulled his wings in close and hoped he wasn't about to die for a man he'd rather spit on than save.

"I'm going to do some inventory." Hanna held up an empty bottle and waved it at Zilly. "It looked like we were running low."

"Yeah, no problem." Zilly didn't look up from the drink she was pouring. "We're not too busy right now. I can handle it."

Hanna didn't need more permission. With Kark and his men gone, the bar was nearly empty, and none of the gang was there to catch her. Jori wouldn't like it, but since Jori was off riding with them, he didn't get a say.

She couldn't think about what they might be doing. She would know if they suspected him of something, if this was some ruse to go and jump him. Hanna kept telling herself that. If they suspected Jori, they'd suspect her. And no one would be letting her walk around unsupervised if they suspected her of something.

Her first goal was the safe. She didn't know how long she had, and she couldn't give an innocent reason for snooping.

She ducked into the closet that held the safe and closed the door behind her, flipping on the overhead light before crouching down in front of it and pulling out the lock cracker she'd retrieved from the storage room.

It wasn't foolproof. Some locks were designed to counteract crackers like this, but those safes were top of the line, incredibly expensive and only released in the last few years. Kark's safe felt old, and even had a few flecks of rust on top of it, like something had spilled and started to degrade the metal.

The lock clicked and Hanna smiled.

Inside there were stacks of credits that probably

came from patrons. Hanna took a picture of the money, but didn't waste time trying to count it.

Next to the case was a leatherbound notebook. It was a few centimeters thick, and the paper was thin. Hanna snapped photos of the pages as quickly as she could, feeling the seconds tick down with every turn of the page. It looked like a logbook, possibly accounts for the bar. Neither the money nor an account book were suspicious things to find in the safe.

The next small notebook she found was written in code.

Jackpot.

Hanna was more careful while taking pictures of these pages, making sure none came out blurry. She'd use the computer at home to try and crack the code algorithmically.

She was about to close the safe when she spotted a small piece of paper sticking out from under the pile of credits. Hanna pulled it out and looked at it with pursed lips.

More code.

She took a picture of the paper and put it back, and then closed the safe back up, sliding her cracker into her pocket.

Hanna stood and took a few deep breaths. She checked the time and saw she'd only spent ten minutes with the safe. Long enough to be noticed, and yet she could have spent an hour and still not done enough.

She hesitated before opening the door. If someone spotted her coming out of the closet, she was toast. But hesitation wouldn't do her any good.

Hanna pressed her ear up against the door to try and listen for other people. She didn't hear anyone. She opened the door and carefully slid out, letting out a breath when she saw the hallway was empty.

One obstacle down.

She looked at Kark's office door and hesitated again. How long did it take to do inventory? Would Zilly come looking for her?

Hanna peeked into the bar. Zilly was chatting with a regular as she cleaned glasses. The place still wasn't busy and the guys were still gone.

This was her chance.

Hanna eased back down the hallway and tested Kark's door. Locked. She'd been prepared for that. She eased two thin pieces of metal out of her pocket and inserted them into the lock. After a moment, she heard a click and was in.

Kark's office was neater this time, no papers scattered on the desk, and the whole place looked like it had been dusted.

Hanna stepped around the small couch beside the door to get to the filing cabinet. These drawers weren't locked, but there was so much paper that Hanna didn't have a hope of making copies of it all.

She scanned the labels. Vendor. Vendor. Bike shop. Vendor. Sex shop. Vendor. Not all business related, but nothing that stood out given Kark's proclivities.

Still, she opened a few of the files and peeked inside, just in case he was hiding anything in plain sight.

The minutes were ticking by fast, and every time she heard a sound come from the bar, Hanna nearly jumped out of her skin.

The other drawers of the cabinet were half-empty, and still nothing stood out. It wasn't shocking. If she were going to hide treasonous documents, they wouldn't be in an unlocked filing cabinet.

Though, if she were doing this, there wouldn't be any documents at her place of business. She was already wary with how much paper she and Jori were keeping at their house. True, paper couldn't be hacked, but it also couldn't be encrypted.

She went to the desk and tried the drawers. Only one was locked, and that was her target. It took longer to pick the lock than it had for the door, which suggested something nicer than a standard desk lock, but Hanna still made short work of it.

The drawer was empty.

Huh?

Why lock an empty drawer?

She jolted to the side, knocking the desk chair out of the way and waiting for the trap to close. A blaster? A camera? An alarm? What was it going to be?

But after several seconds, nothing happened. The drawer wasn't rigged to catch her. It was just empty.

Hanna didn't give up that easily. She stuck her hand inside and felt around, testing for a false bottom, and her work paid off when she touched the back. Not a false bottom, then.

She pulled the drawer out as far as she could and slid the fake backing out to reveal a small compartment with a ring of half a dozen keys and nothing else.

Keys with no lock were useless, but she had dozens of pictures of the pages from the safe. There could be an address in code.

The keys were supposed to be hidden. How often did Kark really check they were there?

Something thumped in the hallway and Hanna jolted into action. She slid the keys into her pocket and grabbed the false backing to slide it back into the drawer, wincing as it tore at her skin.

She closed the drawer, heart beating wildly. She strained to hear, but the door was thick enough to muffle most sound.

And then the knob started to turn.

Hanna had no place to hide. There was no window to jump out of and she was about to be caught in the act. Her eyes darted around, working the problem, until they skimmed over the couch.

She launched herself at it and was pulling the blanket over her as the door opened and Zilly stepped in.

"Are you napping?" she asked, incredulous.

Hanna had to keep her breathing under control, which was difficult given the utter panic that had assailed her. "No, I mean, not really. I'm sorry, is it super busy out there?" She had to sound guilty for getting caught slacking, not spying.

Zilly huffed a laugh. "Not really. But you've been gone awhile and I needed to make sure you hadn't gotten crushed by a pile of crates. Come on. Morn will freak if he knows you were in here. But as far as I'm concerned, that's on him for forgetting to lock the door. I won't tell if you won't. And if you go and clean up the puke in the booth. A couple of kids came in and couldn't hold their liquor."

Hanna made a face and Zilly laughed. "Yeah, I'll get the bucket," Hanna grumbled.

She pushed herself up from the couch and hid her wince as the fabric irritated the wound on her hand. "Are the guys back yet?"

"No, not yet. Come on, I should lock this up behind you. We wouldn't want some nosy customer snooping."

Hanna followed Zilly out and grabbed the mop and bucket from the cleaning closet. Zilly didn't seem suspicious at all, but Hanna couldn't shake the dread of the close call.

Her communicator was burning a hole in her pocket and she was ready to go home and get to work.

13

JORI'S ARM hurt enough that he was starting to worry. The other guys had been hit by plenty of spark and there were bruises, but he and Kark were the only ones bleeding.

Rexx had blood on his boots and flecks on his pants, but none of it was his own.

All Jori wanted was some med gel, a painkiller, and a soft bed. If Hanna was there to fuss just a bit, he wouldn't complain.

He had that weirdly empty post adrenaline hangover that made his hands a bit shaky and the world feel not quite real. The last place he wanted to be was The Docking Station.

But Jursor and Maisum led the gang inside with calls for a bottle of whiskey and for all the rabble to get out. Before Jori took his seat, the bar was almost completely clear of anyone not in Kark's crew. And by the time Zilly put the bottle on the table and Hanna set down a tray of tumblers, the place was empty.

Zilly got one look at Kark and went running for the med kit. She sat it down on the table in front of him and then started tending to his wounds with the seriousness of a battle nurse. Kark tried to push her away twice, but she wouldn't be rebuffed, and when she came back with a wound cleansing spray a third time, he submitted.

Maisum regaled Zilly with the tale of his bravery, apparently fending off a rat the size of a small child while the rest of them fought Fally and his patrons. Zilly giggled at all the right places, but her focus never strayed from Kark.

Did they have something real? Jori didn't understand how anyone could find Kark anything but loathsome. But it seemed that even the worst people could find love.

"Are you alright?" Hanna took the empty chair next to him, her eyes locked on his arm.

Jori looked down, and as soon as he saw the blood, the wound started hurting again. He scowled. "Bar fight. Someone got in a lucky shot."

He reached for the open med kit and pulled it his way. There was plenty of gauze and med gel.

"A knife?" Her voice was cooly professional, but with a quaver of something underneath.

"Broken glass." That moment of the fight flashed back before Jori's eyes, and he winced.

"Let me do that." Hanna grabbed for the gauze as he was turning her way, and her hand brushed up against his wound.

For half a second, nothing happened. Then his vision whited out as he felt power that wasn't his own blast through him.

His wings flared bigger than they ever had, so strongly that he thought they might reach the ceiling. His vision cleared, and Hanna was his mirror, eyes wide and mouth agape, wings twice their normal size for a breath before they shrank back down to what he was used to.

Something clattered to the floor as Jori came back to himself. He slowly looked toward the sound and saw Kark, Zilly, and every other member of the gang staring at them.

Kark broke out into a wide grin. "Bring out the good stuff, Zilly my girl! We just witnessed a Match being made!"

Zilly was frozen in her seat on Kark's lap for

another heartbeat before she bolted up and hustled to the bar, reaching for a bottle on the highest shelf and then grabbing another for good measure.

A Match.

Jori's mind stuttered to catch up. He'd never submitted his data to the Matching database, never particularly cared to find a Match of his own, even if a Matched pair could go far in the military.

Now his Match sat before him, a failed Apsyn spy who was only doing this mission in the hope of gaining her freedom.

A beautiful spy whose eyes were wide and staring at him as if he had some answer she couldn't grasp.

He wished he did. He wished he could find some word to say, something that would make this make sense.

How could Hanna be his Match? How had he not known?

Or had that been the force pulling them together from the very first?

Not every Matched unit was sexual or romantic, but a lot of them were. Could the attraction stem from that? Or was he just looking for excuses?

Hanna broke their locked gazes and reached for the gauze, a wide smile crossing her face. "Can you believe it, babe?" Her voice pitched high and she called him babe, a reminder they were still on the job, they still had parts to play.

He couldn't fail her.

Why was her hand cut?

He choked the question down as he saw her discreetly wipe some med gel across her palm before she tended to his arm. Matches sparked on blood to blood contact, which was why it was rare to accidentally Match. But his wound and her scraped palm were enough.

Zilly poured out shots from a fine Apsyn spirit that glowed faintly red and smelled like flowers. Once Jori's arm was bandaged, he reached out and grabbed his shot.

Hanna took her own and they clinked them together, smiling broadly as they downed the drinks to the cheers of the gang.

Kark launched into a story after that, talking about Vanen and the Matching balls they used to throw before the system of the Match database was founded. Jori tuned most of it out. Kark's obsession with glorified Apsyn history might give insight into his motivations, but that wasn't Jori's job. He was here to find out exactly how Kark was planning to harm Osais and stop him.

Matching wasn't part of the plan.

And it couldn't affect anything.

But as Kark babbled on, Jori reached out for Hanna's hand and turned it over. The med gel was slathered over half her palm and already beginning to knit the slash on her palm closed. It had to itch like mad, but she didn't show it.

Jori grabbed clean gauze and wiped away the excess gel before reaching for a dressing and pressing the bandage over the thin wound. He lightly ran his thumb over the smooth material to activate the adhesive.

Hanna shivered, and it had nothing to do with pain.

He could feel her inside of him. He was used to the power of his spark. It had been with him since he was born. He'd summoned his wings during his first week of life. He knew the exact extent of his power, from how high he could jump and land safely, and how far he could shoot to take out a target.

Now there was a well of power, but it wasn't his. He could feel it, but there was something blocking it, an invisible barrier that he knew he could reach through.

If he dared.

But a Match wasn't a bond. To fully seal the bond with Hanna, Jori would have to reach through that barrier and access her power, and she would have to do the same. If they did that, their combined power would grow exponentially until they were a nearly unstoppable force.

Nearly.

After all, he'd just helped beat a Matched man, though he had no idea where Fally's partner was.

Jori let go of Hanna's hand and looked at the bandage on his own arm. His skin was free of tattoos. Most unmatched Synnrs left an arm bare, just in case they ever found their Match. If he and Hanna bonded, they'd get Matching marks done, tattoos powered by their own spark that lit up the skin like bolts of lightning.

If.

Zilly poured him and Hanna each another drink and Jori knocked his back, even as Hanna drank slower. He had to slow down, he knew. This was the job, and getting drunk put them both at risk.

Already his vision was going a bit wobbly around the edges, and part of him was tempted to pull Hanna close and kiss her, to claim her here in front of the crew.

But he didn't want to share her, didn't want to share the moment.

Almost more than he wanted to kiss her, he

wanted to talk. And wasn't that strange? His prior relationships involved a lot of fun, but not a lot of conversations, and nothing deep. He didn't know if any of his previous partners were looking for Matches, and he was certain none of them were looking for anything serious with him.

That was how he liked it.

Or how he used to.

Now he just wanted Hanna. However he could have her.

Hanna slid off of her chair and onto his lap, wrapping an arm around him and burying her face in the crook of his neck.

"You look like you've been stabbed by a Spark Sword. Now smile and pull me closer." Her tone was even.

How could she be thinking so clearly at a time like this?

But Jori wrapped an arm around her and kissed her neck for good measure.

"Now pick me up and tell Kark we're going home to celebrate." Her arm tightened in anticipation.

Jori stood quickly, kicking the leg of his chair so it fell over. Hanna's legs wrapped around his waist, and he grinned over her shoulder and down at the others.

"This girl needs to be shown just what a Match

means." He squeezed her ass and knew he'd pay for that later, but it made the man cackle. "Sorry, Zilly, my girl might be a bit late for work tomorrow. If she can still walk."

He walked out of the bar, holding Hanna in his arms, and didn't stop until the sounds of filthy laughter faded and all that was left was his Match.

14

HANNA'S BLOOD was buzzing with possibility, and it needed to stop right now. If she concentrated, she could feel Jori's power, could reach for it and use it for her own.

That would be a disaster. They weren't bonded. A Match was only a possibility. And they needed to figure things out before they took any desperate steps.

"How did you cut your hand?" Jori asked once he'd locked the house up for the night.

Hanna had her comm out along with the keyring, but the mention of her cut had her thinking about his injuries. Without saying a word, Hanna grabbed the med kit from the bathroom and set it out on the kitchen table.

"Sit down," she told Jori.

He held up his arm. "It's fine. No need for that."

Hanna flared out her wings and firmed her voice. "Take off your shirt and sit down."

Jori hesitated for another second before pulling his shirt over his head and tossing it to the side. Hanna tried to think professional thoughts, not ogle Jori's body. But she couldn't help but appreciate his muscular chest and strong arms. Her heart tripped over itself, but a few deep breaths had it back under control.

He was her partner and he was hurt. That was all that could matter.

She pulled his arm toward hers and unwrapped the gauze from around the wound. His arm was shiny with med gel and it looked to be healing up well already. Zulir healed fast, especially from flesh wounds, but Hanna had to make sure.

She ran her thumb up his forearm and noted when his skin broke out in goosebumps. He didn't try and pull away. There was a nasty bruise on his shoulder, but that had most likely come from someone's spark. She swiped a bit of med gel over it, though it didn't do much for bruises. She needed to do *something*.

"How could you let someone cut you up?" It came out more accusatory than she meant, but Hanna was barely hanging on. Jori was beaten and bruised and her Match. They were in the middle of enemy territory with only one another to rely on. If she didn't cut him with her words, she might do something reckless, like kiss him.

"I didn't realize he had a shard of glass until he sliced me up." Jori handed her an adhesive bandage from the kit. "That was the only shot he got. I dropped him after that."

Hanna opened the bandage and stuck it to his arm, running her fingers over the smooth surface to make sure it stuck. "What was the mission?"

"Roughing up a rival. Some guy named Fally. I don't think anyone died, but watch out for Rexx. He likes hurting people." Jori switched his grip so that he held Hanna's hand palm up. He ran his hand over the bandage on her palm. "What happened here?"

Her bounty was in the other room, but Hanna made no move to go get it. "I got into the safe. And Kark's office."

His fingers tightened on hers, but he didn't chide her. "And what did you find?" There was a thread of something barely restrained in his voice.

They were both hanging onto professionalism by a quickly fraying string.

"Coded papers in the safe. And a hidden compartment in his office." She flexed her hand in his. "That's where I got the souvenir. I had to act quickly. Zilly nearly caught me. I cut myself sliding the panel back into place."

"Zilly caught you?" Now his grip was tight enough to hurt, but only for a second.

"I convinced her I'd snuck into the office to take a break on Kark's couch. She bought it. We're fine."

"Are we?" He wasn't talking about their cover.

"You tell me." Hanna had no idea where they stood. When the Match flared in the bar, she'd been overwhelmed. Jori had looked blank as stone. He was an ambitious man, a Synnr soldier determined to rise in the ranks. No way would he be happy with the disgraced Apsyn fate had thrown into his path.

She wasn't sure how she was supposed to feel about it. A couple of weeks ago, they'd been nothing but sharp edges and anger. Now she craved the taste of his kiss and wanted to crawl into bed with him and never leave.

But she couldn't tell if that was real or just the intensity of the job getting to her. Hanna had trouble not letting her emotions get involved when she was playing a part.

On her last job as an Apsyn spy, that meant making friends with a young human woman and feeling like dung when it came time to hurt her. Luci had been an innocent bystander, someone Hanna meant to use to make her cover story stronger.

What she felt for Jori wasn't nearly as simple as the possibility of friendship. The chemistry between them was too strong to deny, but she wasn't sure what it meant out of the bed or off the job. What could it mean? She was wrong for him in every way.

And if she bonded with him, she could never go home.

"What is this?" Jori shifted his grip on her hand so that their fingers were laced together.

"You tell me," she repeated.

He squeezed her hand and made a sound of frustration. "Stop playing games! We have to pretend out there." He nodded toward the door. "That's our job, our lives are on the line. In here, I deserve your honesty. You owe me that." She heard desperation in the plea.

"I'm not lying to you. I haven't since we've been on the job." Before that? Well, she couldn't be sure. And she wasn't going to let Jori find some technicality to pick apart.

"You are a spy."

He always clung to that. Hanna pulled her hand out of his grip and started to sort through the med kit supplies and put them back in place. "I'm your partner, and you're just as undercover as I am. Stop pretending."

"You think this is pretend?" His voice was harsh.

Hanna spun towards him. "I don't know, Jori! You kiss me like you're a dying man and I'm offering you life. But when the Match bloomed between us, you were as blank as a starless sky."

"How was I supposed to react? You're Apsyn! You were a spy. Not to mention we were in the middle of Kark's bar and apparently you'd just been caught in his office. I'm not good at this. I'm not good at hiding my emotions."

"I'm not hiding anything." Anger surged through her. She pulled her wings in before she did something foolish, like shoot her spark to make a point.

Jori stepped in close, and if she wanted to back away, she'd need to knock over a chair to do it. "All you do is hide."

How could he think that? She'd been more open with him than she'd been with anyone in years. If there was anyone on this entire moon who knew the real Hanna Karsyn, it was Jori.

He wanted real? Hanna would give him real.

She surged up and captured his lips with her own.

The kiss exploded between them, even stronger than the flare of their Match, or maybe stronger because of it. Heat flooded through Hanna, desperation and need all coiled around the core of her, aching and desperate for more.

Jori's skin was hot under her fingers, and she didn't let herself care about his bruises.

He was getting the real thing from her tonight. No holding back.

Jori hitched her up until she was on the table, the distant noise of the med kit clattering to the floor easy to ignore.

Nothing existed right now but Jori and the intensity of the kiss. It was hypnotic, and the utter surety that she was alive roared through every part of her.

His lips were everywhere, exploring her neck and jaw, while his hands held her waist tightly. The raw thing between them was bigger than desire. His kiss was a claim to the part of her that she kept hidden.

She'd started this, but Jori seized control like it was his to take. And Hanna surrendered it gladly, moaning at the feel of his lips against her skin.

He teased her collarbone, partially obstructed by her shirt, and Hanna wished the thing would burn away to cinders so Jori could take his fill.

Then the beast bit her shirt, getting his sharp canine into the fabric and weakening it until he could tear it in half with his bare hands.

Barbarian.

Hanna loved it.

She was bare to him under the shirt and Jori cupped one of her breasts, thumbing her nipple until she squirmed against him, the bud tightening to a hard point that had her begging for more.

And that more was his sinful mouth. Hanna gasped something out, but if it counted as a word, she couldn't be sure.

Her pants were too tight, the material rough against her sensitive skin. She wanted out of it, wanted to be naked and under Jori while he used his tongue to show her exactly how he felt.

They didn't need words. Not when they had action.

Not when they had *this*.

While Jori worshipped her breasts with his tongue, his fingers tortured her midsection, sliding against skin she'd never before considered delicate and making her gasp at the vulnerability he brought out in her.

She spread her legs wider, begging for more contact, but he kept his attention firmly above her waist, the monster.

She dug her fingers into his sweat dampened hair and could feel his lips curve into a smile around her nipple. But even holding onto him, there was no illusion of control. Jori was setting this pace, and it was Hanna's job to endure it.

She'd gladly endure it every day for the rest of her life.

He pulled away for just a second, long enough to cup her chin and then capture her lips again. Hanna wrapped a leg around his waist and tugged him closer. She could feel the hard length of his cock through his thick pants and wanted more, wanted him naked and pressing into her.

But that would mean breaking the kiss, and she reveled too much in it to let go. Not now. Not when she needed more of him.

He kissed with the skill of a professional, but this time there was an openness to it that Hanna was desperate to keep. She hadn't realized he'd been holding back before, but now all the brakes were off and they were riding wild into something new and dangerous.

Something intoxicating.

She surrendered her whole self to this kiss. There was no way to protect her heart when Jori was kissing her like his was in her hands. Their relationship was supposed to be a ruse, but they'd gone past that a long time ago.

And right now, they couldn't walk it back for anything.

Hanna wouldn't.

He wanted the real her, no lies, no half-truths, no spy games. He had her. And she was determined that they'd still have each other even once this night was over.

There was no pretense now. This was real, *they* were real. And she was going to fight to keep it that way.

Somehow her pants came off. Between the euphoria of the kiss and the bliss of Jori's hands on her, Hanna lost track. But she was naked and spread out on the table for him, his fingers teasing at her entrance.

Braz, she was wet. She could feel it in the tease of Jori's fingers, the way they slid into her with no resistance and stretched her like they were made to be there.

She arched up against him, fingers digging into his skin and urging him on. She was already strung tight, and it would take almost nothing to push her over and through the crashing wave of lust.

Then his cock was there, pressing against her entrance and then in and out, in and out. She moaned around him, taking him fully inside and letting her body get accustomed to the feel of him.

But there was no getting accustomed to Jori. She would never grow tired of this, she already knew it. She wanted him again and again and again. The Zulir sun could explode into a million pieces and she'd still want him here with her.

His body began to vibrate, cock deep in her, buzzing in that particularly Zulir way as he neared his own climax and Hanna clamped down around him.

As she finally crested that wave of pleasure, she called out his name and clung close as he emptied himself inside of her.

She didn't let go as the aftershocks of ecstasy pulsed through her. She'd leave marks on him, she was sure.

Just as he left a mark on her soul.

15

THE BEEPING from Hanna's communicator was an unwelcome intrusion in Jori's ears. Instead of climbing the stairs for round two, Jori and Hanna had collapsed in a heap of naked limbs on the couch, cuddled together and lazily exploring each other as they both slipped into a doze.

It was late, he should have been asleep. But something nagged at Jori, and Hanna's communicator reminded him what.

She jolted out of his arms and snatched her communicator off the table while Jori sat up more slowly. Hanna wrapped the blanket around her naked top while Jori picked up his fallen shirt from the foot of the couch and put it on.

Business again.

Though normally, he was wearing pants when it was time to work.

Jori wasn't sure where his went, so he forced himself to get up and go searching. They were in a pile by the kitchen table along with most of Hanna's clothes. He dressed and then marched the clothes back over to her before sitting back down.

Instead of getting up, Hanna huddled further into the blanket and furrowed her brow, looking at her screen.

"What is it?" Jori asked when it became clear she wasn't going to talk.

She looked over at him with a jolt. "Sorry. I had an algorithm analyzing the images I took from Kark's safe. It just finished. Most of it looks legit, account books from the bar and the like. But one page has an address and a date. Tomorrow morning. Well," she glanced back at her communicator, "I guess technically later this morning."

Jori picked up the keyring from the table and spun it around his finger. "And these?"

"Hidden in Kark's office. Taking them might have been a mistake. I should make copies and then one of us can find an excuse to slip them back where they belong."

"I wish you hadn't gone in without backup." It

was done now, but worry still nagged at Jori. What if something had gone wrong?

"You're the one who was alone with every dangerous person in that gang. Who was going to hurt me? Zilly?" She huffed out a laugh. "She's barely more than a kid and too mixed up in this for her own good."

"You like her." He set the keys back down and leaned back on the couch.

"She's easy to like. Doesn't hide anything, you know. And I mean *anything*. I really wish I didn't know so much about Morn Kark's penis." Hanna shuddered.

Jori choked. "What?"

"She likes to talk about sex. I swear, every day I hear something new about what they're trying in bed. Or on his bike. Or on the couch in his—ew! I hid under that blanket." She made a face and clutched her own blanket around her.

Jori laughed, he couldn't help it. "It's okay to like her."

"The last time I liked someone in the middle of a mission, I nearly got her killed." Now Hanna let go of the blanket and reached for her clothes, offering him her naked back.

"Luci."

"Luci," she agreed.

"She's doing well," he offered. He didn't know the human girl well, but he'd worked with her Match, Ax. "She's back in university."

"That's good to hear." But Hanna didn't ask more, and Jori didn't offer. "We should go to this address."

The change in topic, or rather return to topic, caught him off guard. "And observe the meet?"

"I was thinking we go before, scope the place out. They might be about to hand off weapons or bombs. We don't want to miss that." She placed her communicator on the table and turned back to him. "What do you think?"

He turned it over in his head. "Sounds like something we should call in first."

"It's basically the middle of the night and we're just going to look. Waiting could mean we lose the first lead we've had." Hanna got up off the couch. "Obviously we should send a message on to Solan, but I don't want to wait. It's not like we get backup."

Jori understood the need to move, he could feel it nipping at his own heels. But he didn't want to act rashly. "Are you going to go anyway if I say no?"

"No." She crossed her arms and glared. "I thought we sorted this out. I'm your partner."

She was more than that. His body still hummed with the memory of her, and his blood sang with the potential of their Match. "Fine. You're right. We don't want to miss out on something because we waited. I'll write up a message to Ozar in case something happens to us, then we go."

"Nothing is going to happen to us," she said with the confidence of a soldier about to face her first battle.

Jori wished he felt the same. "Let's get ready."

———

Hanna could have used a bit of extra prep for the mission. She had to clamp her mouth closed around a yawn and wanted to glare up at the sunny sky. There were hours still until the start of the workday, and no one was out except for her and Jori.

They rode together on her bike. Kark and his crew hadn't seen her wheels yet, and they didn't want to risk Jori's ride being spotted. And if this ended in a chase, she didn't want to split up.

Wherever they went, they went together.

Jori held on tight as she weaved through the street on silent wheels. All the lights in the windows around them were out, and she had the strangest sense that she and Jori were all alone on this moon, that if she went into one of those houses, no one would be there.

No one was waiting to wake up. This was their own little slice of the universe.

But in the distance she could see a large truck bumbling towards the highway, and she could hear dogs barking somewhere even farther away. Loneliness was an illusion.

The address led them to a warehouse district that was nicer than the one The Docking Station called home. These buildings had been built in the last few decades and looked like they were power washed to shine white in the sun. The windows had a reflective coating, and none of them were broken.

But there was no gate to stop her from driving into the parking lot outside their destination, and she didn't spot any guards.

"We should hide the bike," Jori's voice piped in through the speaker in her helmet.

"Obviously. Hold on." Rather than pass through the lot as quickly as possible, Hanna took the opportunity to do a few stunts. If there were security cameras, they'd attract attention, but they already had. Hopefully anyone monitoring those cameras would think she and Jori were just out for a joyride.

She took a wide circle around the warehouse before hopping the curb to get back on the road. There was a bus shelter at the end of the street and she pulled in there, hiding the bike under the awning.

Jori had a serious look on his face once he pulled off his helmet. "We're not supposed to waste time doing tricks."

Hanna leaned in and kissed him. That serious look transformed into a hungry one by the time she pulled away, and Hanna smiled. "We deserve a bit of fun. Now come on."

"I didn't spot any guards," he said as they crossed to the back of the warehouse and walked up to the back door like they belonged.

Jori handed her the ring.

There was no guarantee this would work. Just to be certain, Hanna tested the handle first and was unsurprised to find it locked. There was an electronic keypad beside the door, but also a key hole. Hopefully the door didn't require both.

She went through five keys before the sixth finally turned and the door opened.

Hanna was in, with Jori right after her. She looked around for a security panel and found one, but it was disarmed.

"Could be tied to the key," Jori suggested in a low voice.

"I'm willing to take a favor from luck. Now come

on. I want to be clear before that meeting happens. We can leave a camera to catch the action." She didn't need to risk both of their necks just so they could witness whatever was about to happen in person.

They were in a small entrance room, and weak light filtered through around the curtains of a large window. There was a bare desk and computer, along with a chair that was covered in cracked leather and had padding bursting out of the sides. Definitely not as nice as the outside of the place.

The door out of the entry way wasn't locked, but the hallway was nearly pitch black. Hanna activated a flashlight and Jori did the same. Her senses were on high alert, ready for alarms to start blaring or a guard to chase them down, but the whole place felt empty. Hanna would bet an entire credit that they were alone.

The hallway spit them out into the warehouse. It was large enough to fit a couple of land to space vehicles, and there had to either be a huge garage door or retractable ceiling to accommodate that. Currently the central space was filled with tools, gear, and a large forklift.

Around that, the area was lined with storage containers filled with crates. There were two storage levels above them, all open to the central area and packed deep with shelves of their own.

Jori was about to step into the central area when Hanna shot out a hand to stop him. "Don't," she said.

"What's wrong?"

Hanna gave the room a hard look, but nothing stood out under the strong beam of her light. "I don't know. I just don't like how open it is." Anyone with a blaster or mastery of their spark could sit on an upper floor and easily take them out. "Let's try the storage first."

Jori didn't argue. And neither of them suggested splitting up, even if it might have meant they'd cover more area.

The storage area was deceptively big. Hanna had expected a few rows of shelves, but when they turned past one of them, they found an entire section of the warehouse that wasn't visible from the entrance. And here the shelves were positioned like a maze.

Lovely.

They moved methodically. Some of the crates were marked, and Hanna took pictures. Nothing stood out as unquestionably nefarious, so neither of them suggested tugging any crates down to take a look.

Sounds echoed strangely around the room and the light of their flashlights danced along the walls, shelves, and crates, creating a strange kaleidoscope of light and dark.

The sounds bounced off of the storage crates and shelves, echoing in unsettling ways that were hard to pinpoint. Somewhere deep in the warehouse there was a faint noise, a distant percussion that matched Hanna's heartbeat.

The beam of Hanna's light passed over the label on a crate and she froze. "Hold up."

"What?" asked Jori.

Hanna stepped closer to the crate and ran her hand over the thick ink of the marker. It was on the middle shelf. "Help me get this down, I want to see what's inside."

He didn't ask questions. They hefted it down, both barely restraining grunts at the surprising weight. Once it was on the ground, Hanna had to search for a pry bar, but luckily there was one on a hook at the end of the row.

She wedged it into the wood and hoisted the top off the crate.

"*Braznon's bowels*," Jori spat out and glared at the contents of the crate.

Blasters and explosives. A *lot* of blasters and explosives. They were packed tight, with only the smallest amount of padding to keep the material from jostling.

"How did you know?" he asked.

"The logo is from an Apsyn shipping company. I didn't see any other Apsyn logos." Most of the crates were unmarked, and there had to be thousands of them. Was it luck that the one they'd opened was full of deadly ordnance?

Jori pulled an unmarked crate from the bottom shelf and held his hand out for the pry bar. She handed it over and bit her lip while he opened the crate.

Sweaters.

Jori dug in and also uncovered some blouses, but unless weapons makers were getting incredibly creative, the clothing wasn't dangerous.

"Look for more with that logo," he said.

They walked faster, but Hanna didn't see more crates with the Apsyn shipping logo on the shelves. Instead, there was a whole pile of them on a pallet at the end of one of the rows.

But before they could get close, she heard the sound of a garage door slamming open and shot a desperate look at Jori.

Company.

They slunk back into the maze of rows while Hanna strained to hear if that company was coming their way.

She tried to get a count of the crates as she and Jori retreated, tried to get some idea of how much destruction those crates could cause.

It was a lot.

Too much.

But they couldn't do anything about that until they were out of the building. And finding their way back to the entrance was its own problem. Hanna tried to retrace their steps, but when they came to the second turn, she and Jori tried to go separate ways.

They had a silent contest of wills and hand signals, but Hanna wasn't backing down. She was certain of this turn.

The next one, not so much.

They wandered on silent feet for several minutes before Hanna was willing to admit that she might have taken a wrong turn somewhere. And all the while, there was someone else in the warehouse, one unlucky turn away from discovering them.

She was a rat in a maze, and not even a particularly smart rat. A part of Hanna wanted to collapse into a heap and give up. The crates were evil. And possibly moving around of their own volition. Getting caught wouldn't be their biggest worry after awhile. Soon hunger and thirst would get to them, and they'd be lost forever.

Or she was catastrophizing. Being unable to say a word made that easier.

"Hey! Who's there?"

She couldn't see where the voice was coming from, but Jori put a hand on her arm and pulled her back gently.

It might have worked, but he bumped into a stack of crates and sent a loose item on top clattering to the floor.

The sound echoed in the air around them as loud as an explosion. Jori and Hanna stared at each other for a frozen moment.

Then the heat of their assailant's spark blasted their way and they took off running.

16

JORI KEPT a hold of Hanna for as long as he could. Unfortunately, that only lasted until the end of the row when she pulled away and started sprinting.

He followed after. He wanted to shoot his spark back at the hulking figure still shooting at them, but Jori had seen those explosives. One unlucky hit and the entire place would be nothing more than a crater.

He didn't want to burn himself to a crisp, and he certainly wouldn't let anything like that happen to Hanna.

The snare was closing in. Enemy footsteps pounded ever closer, and every turn Jori and Hanna took was further away from the exit and freedom.

They should have called for backup. They should have waited.

But if they had, those weapons could have disappeared, secreted away to whatever contacts Kark had in Osais and already being prepped to bomb more civilians.

There was no right move in this kind of job.

He and Hanna came to a split in two rows.

"Go that way," he told her, a solution beginning to form in his mind. "I'll hold him off."

"What? No!" Hanna looked at him like he was crazy, her spark dancing in her gorgeous eyes. "We can get out of here."

The sound of crates exploding a few rows over was nearly deafening. The acrid smell of dust and small debris assaulted his nose, a mixture of burning wood and melting plastic overlaid with an unyielding metallic tang.

"I'll hold him off," Jori said. He flared out his wings. "Get out of here and call for backup. Tell Major Ozar everything. I'll find my way home."

"You—"

"I'm a soldier, I can handle one thug." Though if that thug made it to the weapons, his chances got slimmer by the second. Jori didn't mention that, but Hanna still looked unconvinced.

"If you die, I'm going to come and steal you from Braznon's grasp, you got it?" She hesitated for just a moment more, and there was another burst of exploding crates.

She ran.

Jori couldn't watch her go, both for the worry that she might not make it and for the small, cowardly part of him that wanted to run with her.

But no. He was buying her time.

He took a deep breath and let the calm of battle settle on himself. There was nothing except the fight. No past, no future. Nothing but now.

The hulking figure stepped into the row, and Jori recognized the wings. Rexx.

"What the *punt* are you doing here?" Rexx demanded.

Jori sent him flying backwards with a shot of his spark.

———

Hanna ran and hated herself with every step.

She recognized Rexx's voice as he and Jori brawled. She was tempted to sneak back and take care of him, but she had to get out and call for backup.

Something in the warehouse was jamming the signal in her communicator, and she had to get clear to get back up. That was the best way she could help

Jori. He was a big bad soldier, he could handle one guy. Even Rexx.

Still, she winced as she heard their clash.

Even though she was looking for an exit, Hanna darted up the stairs when she came to the staircase. She was too stuck in the maze to find her way out, but there were windows up there. That worked just as well as a door for an escape.

She could barely pick up the sound of fighting upstairs, though every few seconds she heard another crate bursting. They had no hope of covering their tracks.

The mission was over.

Almost over. Hanna had to make sure it ended with both of them alive.

She heard something much closer than the fight and spun, wings out and ready to battle, but no one was there.

Then she heard it again. A cry. Pounding.

Hanna turned away from the window and followed the sound to a long, flat plastic crate that was rocking of its own volition. It sat askew from the crates all around it, the rocking having displaced it.

Hanna had a sinking feeling she knew what she'd find, and it made her hurry even faster. The crate was held together with two large metal clasps, but there was no lock. She undid them and hoisted it open.

A young human woman looked up at her with big eyes and panic written across her face. She sucked in a big breath.

Hanna slapped her mouth over the girl's. "Don't scream." She was as forceful as she could be while whispering.

She kept her hand in place until the girl nodded frantically. "Oh god, what's happening, where am I? What's going on? Are you an angel?" The woman's eyes looked beyond Hanna's shoulder to where her wings flared out.

Hanna snapped them in close, but didn't vanish them. If Rexx caught up to her, she'd need them. "My name is Hanna. I'm Ap—I'm Zulir. You're not on Earth anymore, and I have no time to explain." There was a crash from downstairs and Hanna winced. She hoped Jori was winning. "What's your name?"

"S-Sarah," she stuttered from behind chattering teeth. "How—"

Hanna looked around and grabbed a piece of canvas that was sitting on top of more crates, and cursed when she saw they looked just like the one Sarah was in. But they weren't moving.

If there were more humans there, they were still unconscious, and she'd have to deal with them later.

She handed the canvas to the shivering human, who wrapped it around herself tightly.

Weapons were bad enough, but this was even worse. Apsyns, some Apsyns, didn't see humans or other aliens as rational beings. At best they rose to the level of pets. But most Apsyns didn't travel out of the solar system, so any import of humans came through the black market of Osais.

There was another crash. Sarah whimpered.

"Okay, I need you to focus," she told the young woman. "My partner is down there fighting a nasty guy. I'm getting out of here to call for help. I'll take you with me, but you need to be quick and quiet, got it?"

"How can I understand—" Sarah sputtered, stuttering over her words.

"Later." Hanna didn't have time for this. She held up a hand. "Stay here for a second."

Hanna darted back to the window to get a lay of the land. Then she cursed a storm.

She rushed back to Sarah. "Okay, new plan. You stay here and hide in..."

"I'm not getting back in that coffin." Her voice had a surprising level of steel considering the fear in it.

"No, you're not. But if you hear anyone other than

me or someone telling you he's Jori, you stay hidden and you run out of here as fast as you can. Got it? There's a transpo stop just down the street, it's a small structure, three walls, roof, right on the side of the road."

"A bus stop?"

"Sure." Anxiety surged through Hanna. "But give me a few minutes. I'll do everything I can to come back for you."

Sarah nodded tightly and melted back into the shadow. Hanna closed the lid to the crate and turned and ran.

Jori could handle this. He had to ignore the bleeding from his lip, the way his side hurt if he took too deep a breath, and the fact that at least one of his fingers was broken, but he could handle this.

Rexx wouldn't go down.

The man was bleeding in more places than Jori. He was dragging his leg behind him, unable to put all of his weight on it. But he wouldn't fall.

And he had a disgustingly pleased grin on his face, like the punishment of the fight only made him stronger. He barely bothered with his spark, instead relying on his fists and feet. The kicks were fewer now that Rexx had one leg out of commission.

But he was good.

Jori had to handle this.

He blasted out with his spark, but it glanced off Rexx's shoulder as he dodged out of the way, some supernatural sense of when Jori was about to attack alerting him.

Was Hanna gone?

If she was safe, he didn't have to keep holding back. If she was safe, it wouldn't be such a big loss if he had to bring the building down. It wasn't his best plan, but one wrong shot of his spark, one accidental hit of the crates of explosives, and the place would blow.

Jori surged in close and swung his fist, putting all of his fury into the blow. The impact was a sickening flesh and bone thud that reverberated through both of them and sent Rexx reeling.

This time he didn't dodge when Jori hit him dead center with his spark. He dropped.

His chest didn't rise. He didn't twitch.

He was dead.

All Jori felt was the hollow satisfaction that he wouldn't need to take another punch.

He sagged against the nearest row of shelves and

startled when it wobbled a bit. He wrapped his fingers around one of the metal rods that held it up to keep on his own feet.

The floor looked nice and comfortable. He could slide down and sit in a nice heap until the very blood in his veins stopped hurting. That would be nice, wouldn't it?

A blast of a stranger's spark took him in the back of his arm, and Jori jerked around.

Jursor.

Where had he come from?

Jori wrapped his wings around himself to stop more direct hits and pushed himself back into a fighting position.

He could do this all day.

He had to.

Jursor's eyes slid over to Rexx's body, and he let out a bellow of rage. His spark danced on his arms, flecks of lightning growing brighter by the second.

Jori wouldn't be able to dodge, not even with the full force of his spark set to defense. And if Jursor unleashed that power, he'd bring the building down on them, there was no avoiding it.

Not with a fight.

Jori ran.

Or, he tried. His first step was right into a pool of

Rexx's blood and he went down hard, right onto his knee and then his bad side.

He couldn't give up. He wrapped his wings around himself tightly and hoped he could absorb enough of the blow to minimize it.

He strained hard, every muscle tensed as hard as it could be. He heard Jursor bellow, felt the air crackle with an explosion of power.

But the blow never came.

Jori cautiously unfurled his wings and saw Hanna standing over him, wings flared wide and bright, hand held out to help him up.

He took it and struggled to his feet, trying not to wince at the pain in his side. He feared he might have a broken rib, but that was a problem for later.

"You were supposed to get out." It wasn't exactly an accusation, and he couldn't make it a question.

"I saw Jursor's bike. I had to warn you." She vanished her wings and wiggled in under his arm to support his weight.

Jori pulled his wings in tight to keep from shocking her. Then he realized she was his Match. He didn't need to be so careful. His spark was hers.

If they bonded.

Still, a lifetime of discipline kept him in check as Hanna started to shuffle towards the end of the row.

"Weapons aren't the only thing Kark's involved with," she told him as they got to the stairs.

"Isn't the exit the other way?" With the way Jori's body was aching, he didn't want to climb stairs. Riding the bike back home would be bad enough. "*Punt.* We need to do something about the bodies."

Hanna tugged him towards the stairs. "There's something more important."

He could argue. If Rexx and Jursor were found, there would be no doubt their cover was blown. Then again, the contents of the warehouse were enough to put Kark in the loving hands of Synnr Military Intelligence. They'd throw him in a hole and never let him out again.

"What did you find?" he asked between panting breaths. Hanna took even more of his weight, but short of letting her carry him up the stairs, which was not going to happen, he wasn't going to move any faster.

"Sarah, you can come out. It's Hanna, and I have Jori with me." They made it to the top of the steps, and Hanna guided him to a row stacked high with long crates.

A young human woman who had a tarp wrapped around her shoulders huddled, half in shadow, and looked at Hanna like she might disappear if she blinked too hard.

"I don't feel so good." Sarah clutched at her stomach, her face going a bit green.

"Cryo-sickness," Jori guessed. He'd never seen it himself, but he'd heard of it. "We need to get you some food."

"We need to get out of here first." Hanna gently let go of him and crossed to Sarah. "We'll get you somewhere safe, I promise. Can you hold on for a bit longer?"

The girl nodded and then gagged, pulling away from Sarah and bending in half to puke her guts out on the floor at Hanna's feet. After a few heaving hurls, she stood back up and wiped the back of her hand against her mouth. "I'll hold on."

Hanna shot Jori a silent look, one he understood perfectly. Cryo-sickness could turn deadly, and if they didn't get Sarah food soon, she might not make it. "We'll take you to our place and then call in our boss."

Jori eyed the crates. If Sarah had been in one, there was no telling how many were also filled with other humans slowly waking from cryo-sleep.

"No time," Hanna said, keeping her words vague enough that Sarah might not understand.

It killed a part of Jori, but he nodded. It would only

be an hour or two until they could get a proper team to the building.

Outside, an engine roared, and Jori looked out the window. He recognized Kark's bike, along with Maisum and Mardoz. The other two bikes had to belong to other members of Kark's crew.

Kark slid off his bike, took his helmet off, and strutted towards the building, his men following behind him.

It wouldn't take long for him or his guys to spot Rexx and Jursor's bodies.

And Jori, Hanna, and Sarah were trapped on the second floor.

17

"You've got to be fucking kidding me!" The outburst from Sarah had Hanna jolting in shock. The human woman was glaring out the window as Kark and his men made their way towards the entrance.

Hanna understood the sentiment and agreed. Jori was standing up straighter, wings taut and ready for a fight. But he was injured, and they had a non-combatant to protect.

"We can't fight him," she told Jori. "We need to get out of here. Fast."

He looked back toward the stairs, but Hanna only had eyes for the window. She looked back to Sarah and judged her weight. She was a bit shorter than Hanna and had the emaciated look that tended to happen to cryo-sleepers.

Her crazy idea just might work.

"Are they all inside yet?" she asked, joining Jori by the window and looking with her own eyes.

"Just about."

One of the men took up the rear and moved slower, eyes crawling over every speck of the parking lot. But after another moment, he was in. Hanna strained to hear, but the building was too big.

"We've only got a minute to do this, maybe less." Given the state of Jori's injuries, there was no way he could run for their bike and neither could Sarah. But there were plenty of nice fusion cycles sitting right there. "Can you hack one of them?" she asked.

"Not fast enough." Jori spat out a curse.

"That's fine." She thought she heard a sound inside, but she forced herself to ignore it. "I'll carry Sarah down," she said, shooting the girl a sympathetic look. "It'll be a rough landing, but we'll make it. You follow and stand guard. I'll hack two bikes. We ride for HQ."

Sarah needed treatment, but with Kark at the warehouse, they were out of time.

Jori nodded grimly.

Getting the window open was the hardest part. Jori glided down with the grace of a dancer while Sarah held onto her so tight that Hanna feared she wouldn't be able to spread her wings. She managed, barely, and felt the impact of the jump all the way to her teeth.

Sarah threw up again, but that might have had something to do with the jump.

Old habits had Hanna testing the start button before she began hacking, and the first one purred to life. The second did as well. Kark and his men were so confident they hadn't even bothered to lock the starting mechanisms.

Their stupidity was her gain.

Jori gave her one final look before getting on his bike. She wanted to kiss him. Wanted to say something that might... well, she wasn't sure.

But they had to hurry.

Kissing could come later.

She got Sarah on the bike in front of her and engaged the controls. Jori pulled out ahead of her and looked as if he'd been born to ride. She would have been proud if she had any time to feel anything except dread.

How many people were in those crates? What was Kark planning with them? And what about the weapons?

It didn't matter now. This would all be over soon.

In front of her, Sarah felt like skin and bones, her

body quivering against Hanna. Hanna held on tight, but she had to drive fast. Neither she nor Jori had taken the time to sabotage the other bikes. A stupid mistake in retrospect, and one that might get them killed if Kark and his men ran outside.

She couldn't waste time worrying about that now.

Sarah's quivering turned into even stronger shaking before they hit the highway. Under any other circumstances, Hanna would have pulled over.

That wasn't an option now.

The daytime clock had finally chimed, though it was exactly as bright as it had been when she and Jori snuck out at the small hours of the morning. Vehicles clogged the road. If they were in a car, they would be stuck, vulnerable to Kark and his crew.

Instead Jori weaved around where he could, pulling onto the shoulder in more extreme cases. Hanna followed and hoped the other vehicles saw them. No helmets meant that any crash would turn them all into nothing more than bloody meat.

The snarl of traffic unknotted after a few minutes, and she could see the rise of the city center in the distance. Not long now.

And still no chase.

Kark still had a deal to pull off and evidence to hide. He had to know they were coming. When she and Jori got a crew out there, the warehouse could be stripped down to the studs.

That was a problem for later.

She followed Jori at the correct exit and they pulled into the underground parking garage of HQ, blasting past the guard station to the outrage and shouting from the person on duty.

As soon as her bike stopped, Hanna gently eased Sarah out of it. The woman slumped against her, barely standing on her own feet. Hanna carefully tapped her face, hoping to wake her up, but she didn't make a noise or move to indicate she felt it.

Still, Hanna tried to guide her, but whatever strength was propping Sarah up disappeared between one second and the next and she dropped, a dead weight.

"Get me a medic!" Hanna yelled.

That sent Jori sprinting. It was a flurry of motion, guards from the guard station pointing blasters and flared wings, but unsure of whether they should shoot. Another Synnr took a look at Jori and went running towards the building's door.

More soldiers burst out, Major Ozar at the lead. She glared at the guards and motioned for them to lower their weapons.

A medical team took Sarah from Hanna. Hanna

was tempted to follow them. She felt responsible for the girl and wanted assurances she'd be safe.

Under the care of a Synnr military medical team was the safest place that girl could be. Hanna had to let her go.

And she didn't have another choice. "Harek! Karsyn! Report," yelled Major Ozar, "Now!"

———

"This is taking too *punting* long." Jori paced from one end of the small office he and Hanna were holed up in to the other and tried not to imagine a prison cell. He could open that door and walk out into the wider office at any time. There was a bathroom just down the hall and a break room with snacks a little further. No one would stop him.

But if he walked out, he'd keep walking until he found a vehicle and could run back to the warehouse and take care of Morn Kark himself.

Hanna sat staring out the window as if nothing bothered her. Then again, Jori had the uncomfortable realization that she'd spent a lot of time stuck in a very small room. She hadn't even had a window.

"It's been less than an hour since our debrief," she said after a moment.

He wasn't looking at the clock. "Every minute we're here is another that Kark could be stripping away evidence of his crimes."

"And transporting the humans," she added softly.

Jori stopped pacing. "That really bothers you." It wasn't a question.

"Of course it bothers me!" Indignation laced her words. "Why wouldn't it? Doesn't it bother you?"

"But you're Aps—" He cut the word off.

"Seriously?" She pushed out of her chair and turned to glare at him. "I thought we—never mind. Yeah, Jori, I'm Apsyn. It doesn't mean that I'm fine with turning people into pets or science experiments or worse. Besides, we found that girl in Synnr territory. The shipping marks on that crate were for Synnr space. Do you honestly think it's only the Apsyns who bring aliens down to Kilrym?"

He didn't have an answer for that. He was a Synnr, he respected the legitimacy and intelligence of non-Zulir life. Apsyns, as a whole, didn't. He knew that.

And yet Hanna had never been like that. And Morn Kark jumped at every chance to declare Zulir superiority. No human or other alien had dared step foot in his bar, and *braz* like that wasn't supposed to happen in Osais.

Synnrs and Apsyns were both Zulir. They didn't

have some sort of biological difference that informed their prejudices.

They were all just people.

He took too long to answer, and Hanna made a sound of disgust. "You must be glad to get rid of me."

"No!" Jori got it out through gritted teeth, eyes blazing with passion. He stepped in close, so close that he could feel the heat radiating from her body. His fingers ached to reach out and touch her, but he held back. He didn't want her flinching from him.

"Even though I'm a dirty Apsyn spy?" she asked softly.

"Are you ever going to let me live those words down?" A smile pulled at the side of his mouth.

Hanna's expression softened, with a hint of a smile to match his. "Maybe. If you earn it."

But before anything could happen, the door burst open and Solan stomped in, his human Match at his side. She was an intimidating woman, her expression hard and unbending. But when she stood next to Solan, her body angled his way just a little.

"Lena." Jori nodded her way. She was one of the humans he'd helped rescue from Apsyn custody several months ago.

"Jori," she returned.

"The human is in second stage cryo-sickness,"

Solan said, and Hanna flinched, but he continued. "Medics say she'll probably recover. They've got her set up and will transfer her to a hospital as soon as she's stable. We're mobilizing a team right now. We'll have Kark in custody this morning."

"I want in." He and Hanna said it at the same time. Hanna nodded to let him continue. "*We* want in," he said again. "We've been on this guy for weeks. We need to see him taken down."

Lena glanced Solan's way. Jori knew Matches didn't have any sort of telepathy, but from the silent conversation that passed between the two of them, he was willing to believe in magic. Lena finally shrugged.

"It's your call. But you're on cleanup crew. We've already got the breach team prepped and we're not *punting* that up. Let's get suited up."

The four of them strode out of the office and to the armory, strapping into gear with military efficiency.

"Can you get this strap?" Hanna turned her back to him and pulled her hair to the side, revealing a hard to reach fastening over her shoulder.

Jori tugged it tight and secured it, then rested his hand on her back. She leaned into the touch and he breathed deep, taking her scent deep into his lungs. It was embedded in him now, after so many weeks together. Any hint of the floral soap she used would make him think of her.

He wanted it surrounding him. For good.

Solan cleared his throat, and Lena looked at both of them with a smirk.

Hanna broke the contact and Jori finished suiting up, holstering a blaster just in case. "Let's go get this *punting* bastard."

18

Maisum and Mardoz were in custody along with
Andax Wooria, whose name Hanna only learned when
she heard two other soldiers talking.

Kark got away.

She wished she was surprised, but she'd counted
the bikes when she and Jori arrived behind the strike
team. She'd seen four men arrive with Kark. Rexx and
Jursor's bikes had already been there. She and Jori had
stolen two. There should have been five bikes waiting
in the lot.

There were four.

Kark had made it out, and at least one accomplice
was missing.

It wasn't a total loss. Maisum had already begun
talking before he was hauled off to a cell somewhere

deep in a Synnr military facility. The weapons crates were still there, though a few blasters were missing.

The large crates they suspected were filled with people were gone.

Hanna walked through the facility, numbness encroaching on the edges, trying to take her over. Major Ozar had given her an encouraging look. She'd done the job. They'd prevented Morn Kark and his gang of Rebel Demons from using all these weapons to hurt more people.

The job was over.

She was free.

But a bunch of innocent people were still in danger. And Kark was out there somewhere.

She could dwell on that, or she could do her job. Unfortunately, Hanna was exceptional at multi-tasking. She helped a team of techs maneuver a set of crates onto the loading dock where a truck was waiting. All the while, her mind whirred.

Where had Kark gone?

"They'll find him." Hanna nearly jumped out of her skin at Lena's voice.

The human had a set of weapons lined up in neat rows in front of her, a clipboard in hand.

"I know that." Hanna hated the defensiveness she heard in her own voice. "Ozar has all the data we gave her, all of our reports. I'm sure there's already a team heading to the bar. Whatever hidey hole he's in, they'll dig him out."

"But it hurts to leave the job half-done, doesn't it?" Lena stopped counting and gave Hanna a sympathetic look. There was no loathing in her eyes, no secret hate for the reformed Apsyn spy. Maybe Lena didn't know.

Even better, maybe she didn't care.

"He's hurt innocent people. And those girls..."

"You don't know that those crates had girls or boys or anyone else in them," Lena reminded her.

Hanna couldn't accept that. "The crates were identical to the one I pulled Sarah out of. At least half a dozen of them. It's expensive to import people like that. You'd never bring just one."

"I do know that," Lena said. And Hanna remembered a story she'd heard, part of Luci's background, though Luci hadn't been the one to share it with her. Lena and Luci were part of a cluster of humans who'd been stolen away from Earth to be experimented on in Vanen.

Hanna knew about alien importation in theory. Lena had lived it.

"Have you heard anything about Zilly?" That was another thing Hanna was worried about. The girl was caught up in the middle of this and liable to get hurt.

"She's off the grid." Jori came up the row. "Solan was looking for you," he told Lena with a nod back towards where he came.

Lena took off and Hanna waited to see if Jori would say more. He didn't.

"Off the grid?" That wasn't good. If Kark had taken her somewhere, she might already be...

No use borrowing that worry.

"The bar's cleared out. No one at their residence. And neither Kark's nor Zilly's communicators are active. His bike's here, so we can't even try and track that." Jori studied the weapons Lena had laid out. "That's very... neat."

"Ask Lena. I've been moving crates." There was still plenty to do, but Hanna couldn't figure out what was most important. "Does it feel..."

"Unfinished?" he prompted when she trailed off.

"Something like that." All of her emotions were jumbled up. She wanted to launch herself at Jori and cling to him until everything made sense, so, only a decade or thereabouts.

She hadn't finished many missions for the Apsyns before everything went to *braz* and she'd never been stuck on a cleanup crew like this. But she didn't know how to walk away from this one, especially with everything half done.

She yawned. Then she groaned.

Jori stepped in close and wrapped an arm around her. Hanna leaned into him, soaking up his warmth and falling into the feeling of him. "We've been up since early and it's getting late. You missed lunch. Want to get out of here?"

Hanna wasn't hungry. Spending the day deep in the aftermath of Morn Kark's misdeeds had a way of banishing hunger. But she didn't want to walk away. When she walked away, this whole thing would be over.

And what about her and Jori?

She found his hand and took it in her own, giving it a squeeze. "If that's what you want."

The bikes had been impounded and they'd come in a large van with the rest of Solan's squad. But her own bike was still hidden at the bus stop down the street, and they found it waiting for them.

It might have been her bike, but Jori took the controls. She held on tight as he powered it up and pulled them away from the warehouse and all the responsibilities that would be waiting for them tomorrow.

She didn't tell him where to take her, and she

wasn't surprised when she realized where they were going.

Their place.

It probably wasn't safe. Then again, Kark couldn't know they were the ones to betray him. She hadn't seen any cameras or other surveillance in the warehouse. Rexx and Jursor were dead, they couldn't say who killed them.

And Kark was on the run. Chasing them down would put his own freedom at stake.

When Jori pulled into the driveway, he gave Hanna a questioning look. He knew the risks just as well as she did.

This was their place. It wasn't real. They'd need to move out in a day or so anyway. But it was where they were together. She didn't know how they could exist as a pair outside in the real world.

Jori was still a soldier. She was still a disgraced ex-spy. They hadn't said a word to each other about their Match. And she wasn't going to break that silence tonight.

But she needed another stolen moment with him.

Hanna nodded.

Jori stored the bike in the shed and they both headed inside, sparks at the ready in case the place was compromised and they'd need to fight.

It was as silent as ever. Clean, too. They'd both been diligent about hiding any incriminating evidence or papers whenever they weren't using them.

Hanna took Jori's hand and led him up the stairs to their bedroom for one last time.

———

Jori thought he should say something. The heavy weight of the future, of the road they'd need to choose, sat on his shoulders.

Then Hanna pulled her top off and he forgot every language he'd ever tried to learn.

His mouth went dry. His blood heated. And his cock perked up, ready to take control.

She smiled at him, something sweet and sultry that made him want to get on his knees and beg. Instead he surged forward and captured her lips with his own.

Hanna took his kiss and moaned for more, her heat and passion wrapping around him like a blanket. There was a gentleness here, a vulnerability she'd never let him see before, and Jori cherished it.

His fingers brushed over the exposed skin of her neck, and she shivered under his touch, tilting her chin up and silently begging for more. The kiss shifted, deepened, and his arms snaked around her waist to pull her even closer. He savored the taste of her, savored the hot press of her body in his embrace.

Every nerve he had came alive as their tongues brushed together—exploring each other with the intensity and care they couldn't have allowed themselves before now.

Her fingers teased the edge of his shirt, and he allowed her to pull it over his head. Her breasts pressed against his chest as she kissed him again, a luscious temptation he didn't want to resist.

He palmed one, his fingers pinching a nipple just strong enough to make her gasp and give him one of those tantalizing moans he never wanted to forget. Hanna didn't hold back anything tonight. All of her responses were his, and he'd savor them like nothing else.

Hanna pulled away, and he let out a groan the moment that connection was severed. Her smile was beyond wicked, and she reached down to the button on his pants, her fingers teasingly stroking his rock hard length until he was arching against her.

Then she undid the rest of the buttons and dropped to her knees in front of him.

Punt.

She grinned up at him, her expression somehow

caught between some holy celestial spirit and demonic temptation. Then her tongue darted out to lick her lips, and it tipped the balance.

Demonic temptress. All the way.

And he'd gladly follow her into damnation.

As if sensing his need, Hanna slowly drew her fingers up and down his length, her touch light and so, *so* demanding. She looked up at him through thick lashes, and Jori lost himself in the intensity of her gaze.

Desire blazed hot and strong between them. He wanted to feel every inch of her wild passion, wanted to revel in every bit of pleasure they could eke out of one another.

And he never wanted to let it go.

Her fingers teased him further with each gentle stroke, and the sounds he made couldn't have come from his throat—desperate, needy, completely under her thrall. His own fingers curled into fists to keep from digging into her gorgeous hair and taking control of this moment.

The heat of her breath brushed against his skin before she sucked him into her mouth, and Jori's world tilted until he lost his balance completely and yet still managed to remain standing.

Hanna's mouth around him made him powerful

and vulnerable at the same time. It was a precious gift he couldn't resist. He couldn't do anything but surrender to the way she took him and be happy for it.

He was close to the point of no return. He could feel it gathering, could feel his shaft beginning to vibrate with that unique Zulir pleasure, and Hanna knew it too.

The evil temptress gave him a final lick and pulled back, lips wet and red and swollen.

So *punting* perfect.

Jori dragged her back to her feet and kissed her hard, claiming that smile that he already knew he'd adore forever. Now he only had to find the way to make it so.

He stepped out of the fallen heap of his own pants and backed Hanna up against the bed. His cock was insistent, craving the tight heat of her sex and all she could give him. He wanted her writhing around him, calling his name and saying those words that even he hadn't yet managed to utter.

Instead he lay her down and undid her pants, pulling them off and getting her just as naked as he was. She sprawled on the bed like it was a sensual altar, legs open, breasts heaving, lips swollen, skin flushed.

Perfect.

His.

He could feel the heat of her spark deep inside of him, and Jori was tempted to summon it, to seal the bond between them so that neither one of them could walk away. He knew his own heart, knew what he wanted.

But he forced that emotion down. Not now.

Now yet.

Instead he buried his face in the juncture of her thighs and feasted on her heat. He inhaled the musk of her arousal, the sultry fragrance that somehow had him by the cock. Hanna groaned in time to his hungry tongue, her body writhing under him, fingers digging into his skin.

Desire burned hot and bright enough to leave a mark on him, body and soul. It burned more than just a memory into his spirit. He fed off her pleasure, needing to give more for every moan and sigh.

His own cock was hard as a rock, and if he didn't get inside her soon he feared he might explode, possibly into a billion tiny pieces. But this was about her pleasure, about her ecstasy.

And Jori was nothing if not thorough.

Hanna rocked against him, his name a prayer on her lips. She cried out, body rippling and writhing as she came.

He'd remember the sound of her, the taste of her, forever. And he pulled away just enough to watch her surrender to abandon, his fingers still teasing her as she shivered.

Their gazes locked. Her spark danced in her eyes, electricity close enough to the surface to dance along her arms and make her hair begin to stand on end. Jori knew he had to be the same, hanging onto control by nothing but a thread and desperate for more from her.

He found her entrance with his cock, pushing in, gaze never leaving hers. It was almost too much, the tight, wet heat of her. She wrapped around him and he couldn't hold on.

Jori let go of whatever was left of his control, thrusting into her with a groan. He savored each of her moans and sighs as he moved faster and faster, the need to make this last and the need for release warring for dominance.

Hanna found her peak again, her body shuddering around his, and he was lost. His cock vibrated madly with every thrust until he couldn't take the sensation anymore and found his own release, emptying inside of her and chanting her name until he was completely spent.

He pulled her close after that. The bed was a bit

askew, the covers on the floor somewhere, and they'd managed to overturn a lamp.

And yet the turmoil of the room had nothing on the turmoil in his heart.

"What are we going to do?" Hanna asked quietly, her lips ghosting over his collarbone.

Jori didn't have a complete answer.

All he knew was he wasn't letting Hanna go.

19

Hanna knew she should pack up her things and go, not that there were many things to pack. The house had been stuffed full of set-dressing for their cover. The decorations, the dishes, even the clothes weren't hers.

All she would miss was the bike.

And Jori.

She groaned in the middle of folding a jacket and let it fall to the bed. He was in the shower, and it wouldn't take any effort for her to shuck off her clothes and join him in delaying the inevitable.

She'd woken early and had the cowardly thought that she could sneak away. Then she'd realized that Jori was lying awake right next to her.

Then sneaking was the last thing on her mind.

She'd fallen for him. All the signs were clear. She'd

let him get past her defenses and burrow himself deep in her heart.

Had she told him that?

Of course not!

For all the intensity of their sex, he hadn't said anything about forever, or even next week. Neither of them had brought up their Match. It was like every time they flirted up against needing to talk, they fell into bed or the job.

And instead of talking now, Hanna wanted to run.

It was too risky, and she was done living her life on the spark's edge. She wanted something safe, or if not safe, at least uncomplicated.

Was that so much to ask?

She didn't want to get all caught up in a guy who'd resent her as soon as the hormones cleared away, love or no.

The room wasn't helping. If she let herself think about the bed for more than three seconds, she'd remember the feel of Jori's lips on her skin, his fingers making a mark of their own.

Whatever. The jacket wasn't hers, anyway.

She headed downstairs and pulled out her communicator where she still had pictures of the files she'd copied. No doubt she'd have to erase them soon enough, but if Kark and Zilly hadn't been found yet, maybe she could do something to help.

She set her communicator on the table and engaged the holo-projector function so she could look at bigger versions of the documents and keep all of them in front of her.

It didn't take long for words and numbers to blur together. Hanna lost herself in the work so much so that she startled when Jori tromped downstairs.

"What are you looking at?" he asked. His hair was still damp, a drop of water clinging to one of the curls he hadn't managed to wrestle into submission. He wore a simple outfit of dark pants and a green long sleeved shirt, and completed it all with a pair of boots.

Hanna was staring and she knew it. Still, it took several seconds for her to pull her gaze away. She'd seen him naked. She'd had his cock in her mouth more than once. So how could he still light her up like this?

"I'm giving the documents another look," she explained. "Just in case there's some hint of where Kark might be hiding away." Those words tugged at her subconscious, and Hanna tried to chase the thought, but it went nowhere.

"No doubt Ozar has a dozen techs working these documents too," he pointed out.

Hanna shrugged. "I'm one more set of eyes. And we know him better than the techs."

"You could head into HQ and offer your expertise."

Hanna didn't have a response for that. She could. She probably should. But she kept scrolling through her documents, batting one aside once she was done with it to look at the next.

No answers.

"When do you have to go in?" She tried to sound light, as if her heart didn't weigh three tons. "Job's over, right?"

"It's wrapping up." He hadn't moved a centimeter, but she could feel his eyes on her. "I haven't been given new orders yet. I'm sure someone will come looking if I don't report in by next week."

"Want to find a beach and spend a few days there?" It was supposed to be a flirty joke, something so clearly outrageous that they couldn't do it. Why did it sound plausible?

Jori crossed the room in three steps and wrapped his arms around her tight. Hanna returned the hug with a desperate sob, clinging to him as if he was her only anchor to the world.

"Name the place," he said, with surprising fierceness.

Hanna had to let him go and step back, to put

distance between them and regain her composure. And she would.

In a minute.

Or an hour.

She clung tighter. They breathed together, heartbeats in sync, as close as they could be while they were both fully clothed.

"I don't want this to end when we walk away." Jori had his hand on the back of her neck, the grip tight but more comfortable than controlling. "Tell me what I have to do."

That earned him an indignant laugh. "You?" Now Hanna really did have to pull away. "You're the perfect soldier, remember? I don't want to pull you down. If you... if we... I can't be your Match." It hurt to say. It was the dream of every Zulir to find their Match, to bond and fall in love and do everything the fairy tales said were true.

Jori didn't respond to that. He looked away from her, eyes snagging on the papers floating above the holo projector. Then he shook his head violently. "Damn that to *braz*. I love you."

"What?" Shock ripped through her, a mix of joy and fear and denial. "What?" She had to repeat it, brain refusing to completely process the words.

Jori moved back towards her, slowly this time,

giving her plenty of opportunity to move out of his way. "Is that so hard to believe? I thought..." He took a deep breath. "That doesn't matter. I love you. Match or not. I want to be with you, I want this to be real."

He reached out and cupped her cheek. Hanna couldn't help but lean into it, eyes falling closed as she soaked up the sensation. "I can't be the ruin of you." Tears threatened to fall, but she squeezed her eyes even more tightly shut. "I've hurt too many people."

Jori didn't let go.

Hanna grabbed for his arm but didn't pull it away. She held on. "Don't let me ruin you."

He kissed her. It was soft, sweet.

Loving.

Hanna had no defense against it. She clung to him, afraid that when this moment was over, Jori would come to his senses and realize he had to walk away. If this went on for much longer, she wouldn't be able to hold her words back. And if she said it to him, it was all over.

They could exist in this little house, in this time outside of their normal lives. But when they got back, when Jori was with fellow soldiers, he'd remember who she really was. And he'd hate her.

That gave Hanna the strength to pull away and turn from his kiss.

She stared at the files ahead of her, looking for anything that would keep her from turning back to him. She could still feel Jori breathing behind her, his presence too big to ever ignore.

Then she saw the picture.

Hanna reached for the projection of the file and expanded it. It was a photo of Kark's desk, one she'd taken just in case she needed to put it back in order. And on the corner of the desk was a picture of a fusion cycle. That wasn't what she was looking at, though. It was the background.

"What is it?" Jori asked, back to business.

"I think I know where Kark is."

———

Jori called it in. Solan let him know the tip would get checked out, but there were half a dozen other more likely locations to look at first. It could be a week before anyone looked at Kark's little hideaway.

The old Jori would have left it at that. Maybe he would have pressed Solan to take things further, to bump it up the list, but eventually he would let it lie.

But this mission had changed him in ways he was only beginning to understand.

"We can't just let him get away!" Hanna scowled

when he gave her Solan's response. "He could hurt Zilly. And get away!"

"We're not letting him, let's go." It was rash. Reckless. Just like the day before when they charged the warehouse without backup. But that turned out alright. With Hanna by his side, he felt like he could do anything.

Even if she didn't love him.

Jori had never uttered those words to a lover before, had never even come close to considering it. It had been almost easy to say them to Hanna. And crushing not to hear them in return.

He understood her reluctance. It was his own thrown right back in his face. Was this some kind of cosmic retribution? He'd played fast and loose with the hearts of too many people to count. This was the payback.

But Hanna looked at him the same way he knew he looked at her, like it would still be bright as day in the darkest nights of winter as long as he was with her. There was a depth of longing in her expression that she never quite hid when they were alone.

He hadn't let himself believe it at first. Was it possible she returned his feelings?

There was no time to ask. They suited up for the ride, clad in leather and ready to face an army.

They pulled their bikes out of the shed and powered them on. Hanna gave him a final nod before pulling on her helmet and climbing on her ride. He put his own helmet on and did the same.

Hanna took the lead. She'd found the address of the hideaway in Kark's files, but knew about it from Zilly's endless talk about her relationship with the man. The cabin was secluded outside the city and near enough to a large salt flat that was perfect for pushing a fusion bike to the edge of its capabilities.

He was already riding faster than he would, but Hanna controlled her bike with the steady hand of a professional, and she was trusting Jori to keep up the pace. The road rolled by under them, the wind battering his jacket, and he wished he could let go and enjoy this.

There was a certain pleasure to riding their bikes like this, speeding along in a way they'd never be able to in a closed vehicle.

It was almost like flying.

When he'd been a boy, Jori had been determined to be the first Zulir to use his wings to truly fly. It didn't matter that it was physically impossible, he was going to do it.

He'd been so determined that he'd jumped off the

roof of his school. His wings had slowed his descent, but they hadn't prevented the broken leg.

He'd been chasing that excitement, that need to fly ever since.

When this was over, he was going to have Hanna teach him even more tricks for the bike. She knew the secrets and he'd seen her pleasure in teaching him.

All he had to do was convince her to love him first.

And survive long enough to make it worth it.

He put his head back into the drive. It would all be for nothing if this ended up in a crash of gnarled steel and smoke before they even reached their target.

The road was surprisingly crowded heading out of the city. He and Hanna had to weave around vehicles and make their own path on the shoulder or share lanes with other drivers. Far from safe, but time was of the essence.

Hanna turned off the highway after another few minutes, taking an exit that was mostly deserted. They were officially out of the city now, and this was no spot for tourists or vacationers.

Except for Kark, he hoped.

The green trees that ringed the forest around Osais started to fall away for more rugged terrain. The trees were shorter here, stumpier and browner. But mostly it was scrubland and shrubs with foothills off in the distance.

Not exactly Jori's idea of a beautiful nature getaway, though perhaps there was some spectacle in the starkness.

He felt exposed. He and Hanna were the only two people on the road and had been for some time. The spot between Jori's shoulder blades ached as if he had a sniper's eye on him, but there was no good vantage for a sniper anywhere near him.

Hanna took another turn, this one down the barest suggestion of a road. Shrubs and scraggly branches competed with gravel to make a path, and they had to slow down to barely more than a crawl.

He was tempted to suggest walking the rest of the way, and Hanna must have read his mind.

She pulled off the road and he followed.

"We're close. I want to stay off the road." She pulled off her helmet and stashed the bike as best as she could. Jori followed suit.

He wanted to warn her to be careful or something equally ridiculous, but that would earn him a glare and he'd deserve it.

His spark lit his veins, ready for anything. But the walk was almost pleasant. He could hear birds chirping in the distance, and small animals scampered through the bushes. They didn't care that a saboteur might be hiding from justice only a few meters away.

They reached the end of the cover, and Hanna held up a signal to stop. They kept low, but the terrain didn't offer much cover.

If they were spotted...

Jori began to reach for his communicator. Maybe he should have told Solan they were going.

Then there was movement, and he stilled his hand. Whoever it was, they were too far away for Jori to tell if it was Kark.

"I'm calling this in," he whispered to Hanna, and she nodded.

But before he could reach for his communicator again, a bird squawked wildly and a burst of spark incinerated the shrub right next to his head.

20

Hanna dove for cover, summoning her wings and wrapping them around herself before she could fully assess the situation. Her eyes landed on Jori first, and the wave of relief she felt when she saw he was alive was only challenged by the tsunami of anger that anyone would dare hurt him.

He was hers.

She recognized Wrake and Malo from the bar, but they'd never spoken. The men were hangers-on, usually relegated to the far end of Kark's table and desperate for his approval. Clearly they recognized her and Jori right back. They didn't look surprised, but she didn't care.

She lashed out, her spark a whip aimed straight at Malo's face, but he managed to block it.

The smart move would be to take the defensive position. Find cover, hit where she could, and call for help. If she and Jori planned it right, they might even be able to cover enough ground to make it impossible for the bikers to advance.

But she was angry. And she was done playing it safe.

She focused her energy into her wings, building up a defensive wall of her spark that would take a *punting* cannon to blast through, and launched herself at Wrake.

Jori had his fire focused on Malo. She had to trust he could take care of that.

The tip of her wing brushed against Wrake's, and lightning sizzled in a battle of pure energy. He was no weakling, and Hanna had to pull her wing back before he managed to damage her. But while he was distracted, she hit him with a lick of power and smiled in satisfaction as he yelped.

There was a purity to fighting, something she'd never find in spy work. Her enemy was right in front of her. He was trying to kill her. She had to put him down first.

But *punt*, the man was powerful. If his wings were any bigger, she might have thought he was Matched.

Hanna couldn't afford to look over at Jori. He was

a far more skilled fighter than she was. He could handle himself.

Wrake battered her with strike after strike of his spark, so strong it started to reverberate through her wings and make her ache. She couldn't take this forever. Her wings weren't a muscle. They didn't tire. But eventually she'd run out of energy.

Hanna had to end this. And though there was a purity to fighting, dirty tricks got the job done.

The next time Wrake hit her, she fell back with a cry, careful to keep herself shielded but holding her wings limply.

Wrake couldn't resist the fallen target.

Instead of doing the wise thing and finishing her off from a distance, he came in close. And when he was right over her, Hanna struck, sending a blast of her spark straight to his exposed neck and watching as he fried.

He dropped.

She stood.

Jori was looking at her, face a mask of horror. But then it cleared and he ran at her. He didn't hug her, they didn't have time, but the relief was clear.

"I thought he got you," he said.

Hanna couldn't resist poking at the old wound between them. "Dirty spy trick."

"Thank the gods for that." He squeezed her hand, and then they were heading towards the cabin.

Morn Kark blocked their path.

His eyes slid past Hanna to glare at Jori. "You're a dirty traitor?" Kark spat the word, his scowl impressive.

"I think that's you," was Jori's response.

Both she and Jori were worse for wear from the fight against Kark's men, but the two on one odds were in their favor.

Except they needed Kark alive.

Killing a target was easy. There was no need to hold back. Fighting not to kill was like doing it with one arm and half a wing.

"It's over, Kark," Jori said. His wings were flared as wide as they could, spark crackling and ready to burst. "I'm taking you in."

Kark threw his head back and laughed, the sound a rumble of thunder. "It hasn't even begun, you *punting ynstit*."

Hanna scanned the property behind him. She didn't see any movement, but Kark was so confident, she worried he had someone covering his back.

Was Zilly there? Was she alright?

The questions were on the tip of her tongue, but

Jori was doing the talking and she wasn't about to let Kark know she cared.

"Then tell me all about it," Jori invited.

Kark took a step to the side, and she and Jori mirrored him. Tension rose with every centimeter they moved.

Hanna stepped away from Jori, moving to cut Kark off from the main path. She didn't want him running, not that there was any place to go out in this wasteland.

"Who cares about one little warehouse? We're bringing this defiled moon back to order. We'll cleanse it, and it will be welcomed back into the Apsyn embrace." His face was bright with conviction, his own wings jerking as he spoke.

Hanna couldn't keep her own scowl off her face. The man had never even been to Kilrym. He knew nothing about regular Apsyns, as if they cared about what went on with the Synnrs or wanted more war. But there was no trying to convince him, and no need.

He'd made his choices.

She made hers.

Hanna lashed out with her spark and caught Kark in the side. But it wasn't enough to take him down. He shot at Jori and then surprised her by striking out in two strands of spark, something only the most skilled of Zulir ever managed.

Hanna took a hit to the hip and sank to one knee, but shot right back at Kark's legs. That sent him tumbling. And unlike when she did it, it wasn't an act.

She and Jori were relentless, keeping him covered by a rain of electric power that he couldn't hope to fight. And when they advanced on him, Kark was defiant, blood flecking against his nose but otherwise not very injured.

"For the true king of the Zulir!" Kark screamed, before his eyes went white with a burst of lightning.

He'd turned his spark inward and killed himself rather than be captured.

Jori cursed and slapped the ground next to Kark's head.

"At least he didn't get away." Hanna tried to keep up the good attitude. With three bodies on the ground, it was hard to sound convincing.

Jori yanked his comm out of his pocket and spat again. "No signal. How is that even possible? I need to call this in. At least now they can call off the search for Kark."

"Someone might be jamming it," she suggested. "And we don't know if anyone else, if Zilly, is here."

"Start looking for her and keep your guard up. I'm

going to see if he has anything on him and I'll catch up."

To *braz* with decorum. Hanna leaned in and kissed Jori, the joy of the win and the frustration at Kark's death needing to be tempered by the feel of Jori's lips.

She reluctantly pulled away and stood. "Let's finish this."

———

The main cabin was set back behind a parking area, and there were two smaller dwellings even deeper into the scrub. Hanna counted two bikes and one large vehicle with a covered trailer attached to it.

Three men accounted for. Unknown how many were left.

She moved carefully, wings held in a defensive position and ready to respond to an attack.

But the attack didn't seem to be coming.

Hanna ducked beside the trailer to get a better look. She didn't spot movement. Maybe Wrake and Malo were the only backup Kark had.

She hoped Zilly wasn't dead.

The fear tried to crush her. Hanna had messed up enough in her short career, and she didn't want to pile one more failure on top of it. As stupid as it sounded,

Zilly felt like some sort of cosmic redo of how she'd treated Luci. Hanna had hurt that human, she'd nearly killed her.

Zilly was another innocent caught up in something bigger than herself. Maybe this time Hanna could save her.

It didn't matter that ultimately Luci had turned out fine. Hanna's actions had nearly gotten the girl killed more than once.

No more stalling.

Hanna headed for the main cabin and kicked the door open.

Zilly threw her hands up and screamed. A flash of spark hit the door beside Hanna and she dodged to the side.

"It's me, Zil! It's Hanna. I'm here to help." She had to keep her own wings up to prevent damage from the young woman's erratic fire. After a moment, it slowed and then stopped. Hanna risked lowering her wings and took in the sight of Zilly.

It was better than she feared, but still not great. Zilly didn't appear to be bruised and she wasn't tied up, but she was cowering on the floor, the neckline of her shirt stretched and beginning to tear as if she'd been pulled around.

Hanna wanted to rush in, but she forced herself to take in the room.

There was a bed off to one corner, the sheets rumpled in a telltale fashion. A small suitcase had items bursting out of it at the foot of the bed, mostly full of masculine clothes that Hanna would bet belonged to Kark.

A half full bottle of whiskey sat on the table with two glasses.

It all might have been evidence of a nice vacation, if it weren't for the sobbing woman on the floor.

"Han-na?" Zilly hiccupped her name and pulled her legs in tight, making herself even smaller. "He—it—what's going on?"

Satisfied no one was going to jump her, Hanna fully entered the cabin and crouched down next to Zilly. "Jori and I are here to help. Come on." She reached out to help her up.

Zilly ignored her hand, and tears fell further down her face. Her wings flashed, disappearing for a second and then coming back, as if she couldn't concentrate on maintaining them. "Why? Did Morn ask you to come? Where is he?"

Braznon's bowels. Did the girl not get it? Frustration warred with concern, and Hanna didn't know what to say. How could Zilly not know what was going on?

Then again, if Kark had burst in on her and demanded they leave without any more information, why would she?

Hanna was done with lying. "Kark's been mixed up in some bad stuff. You don't need to go down with him."

"What? How do you know that?" She wasn't looking at Hanna now, curled even further up and holding her hands tight to her chest.

This was going to destroy her. If Kark wasn't already dead, Hanna would kill him herself. Zilly didn't deserve this, no one did.

Distantly, Hanna heard the firing engines of some kind of vehicle. Had Jori managed to get a message out to HQ? That was fast.

And where was he?

Tendrils of unease unfurled in Hanna's belly. Something about this felt wrong. Jori should have been here by now. Even if he'd stripped Kark down to his underwear, it would have only taken a few minutes.

And how had HQ missed this place? They had the exact same information she and Jori had. It should have stood out as an obvious hidey-hole.

She and Jori had approached the entire mission as

if Kark was acting alone. What if there was a bigger conspiracy?

That was a problem for later. Right now, she had to get Zilly somewhere safe. They could worry about massive Apsyn schemes when they were on safe territory.

"Why are you here, Hanna?" Zilly asked again, voice growing stronger. "Aren't you Apsyn?"

"I'm here to stop more people from getting hurt. We need to get you out of here." She offered Zilly her hand again.

The girl took it, but barely tried to stand. Hanna had to yank her up.

"Where's Morn?" she asked, eyes darting around.

"He's dead." No sense lying when she might see his body on the way out.

Hanna was prepared for hysterics. What she wasn't expecting was the way Zilly froze. "Dead?" Her usually expressive voice was flat.

"He killed himself rather than be captured." Should she offer condolences? She wasn't sure of the grief etiquette when the dead lover was also a traitor.

"Fanatics are always eager to die for the cause."

Hanna barely had time to process that sentence before Zilly's spark flashed in front of her and she fell unconscious to the ground.

21

Jori woke up with his hands tied behind his back, shoulders wrenched into an agonizing position. The last thing he remembered was hearing a ship landing.

Hanna.

Her name was enough to jolt him to attention. He opened his eyes fully and scanned the room. It was tiny, little more than a closet, with only a small stream of light coming in through a poorly patched broken window high on the wall.

Hanna was slumped on the wall opposite him. Her chest rose and fell slowly, and that was a relief. She was alive. As long as that was true, they could get out of this.

If anything happened to her...

No. He refused to think it.

She groaned, and her head lolled to the other side before she blinked her eyes open. Their gazes locked. Then she scowled. "Zilly was in on it."

He nodded. "She has reinforcements."

He struggled against his restraints, but they were tight and competently tied. Maybe he could use his spark to loosen them, but he didn't want to risk it just yet. Hanna's own hands were tied in front of her, and she worked on the rope with her teeth. After a minute, she gave up and let her hands fall into her lap.

They were done. Major Ozar didn't know where they were, his comm was lying broken on the salt next to Kark's lifeless body, and it would be days or longer before anyone thought to check this place out.

He and Hanna would be long dead by then.

"I'm sorry." It was all he could think to say.

Hanna's face screwed up in confusion. "For what?"

He looked pointedly down at her bound hands and then back up. "For getting you into this situation."

"We got into this together, babe. And we're—" She snapped her mouth shut as voices rose on the other side of the door.

"This is a screw up of epic proportions!" It was Zilly's voice, but in a sharper tone than Jori had ever heard. She sounded hardened, not at all like the bubbly bartender who'd befriended Hanna.

"Do not take that tone with me." The second voice belonged to a man and was tinged with the tones of Kilrym. An Apsyn.

"Father—"

"No," he cut Zilly off. "You should have had this under control a long time ago."

There was a screech along the ground as something heavy moved. "I had that ogre on a tight leash, just as you instructed." Some of her sharpness softened. "He would have wasted everything we gave him on useless attacks and had us captured by the authorities in a matter of weeks."

"Get me a drink." Her father sounded tired. Jori had no sympathy for the man. "How did you let the agents get so close?"

There was a long pause before Zilly spoke. "Hanna sounded like one of us. I thought she was grifting that soldier, maybe trying to get some information. She never said anything that favored the bloody Synnrs."

Jori's gaze snaked over to Hanna at that. She was working on her bindings again and paused to give him a bit of a grin.

No, she certainly wasn't running a grift.

"At least we retrieved our payment, so this wasn't

a total loss. I have my men stripping our hideaways. We'll be out of here in two hours. Have you killed the agents?"

There was another pause, and something too faint for Jori to hear.

"*Braznon's bowels*, girl! Do your job." He sounded more like a man chastising a misbehaving employee than a father talking to his daughter.

"We should bring them with us," Zilly said, sounding a bit frantic. "As hostages."

Even through the door, Jori could feel the tension in the air. "Explain."

"We're going to get out of this, some ordnance short and bodies on the ground, but we're clear. Next time that might not be so. If we keep them alive, we'll have something to trade for our freedom." The words tumbled out fast, as if she was making it up on the spot.

The woman might be the mastermind of Kark's operation, but maybe she didn't want to get her hands bloody.

"Keep the Synnr, we're not letting an Apsyn traitor live." Then there were footsteps as he left the room.

Jori stared at the door. His hands were behind his back, but he could still use his spark. He was running low on energy, but there was enough for this. Enough for Hanna.

Tension ran tight in every muscle as he strained. But Zilly didn't approach the door. And a moment later, her footsteps retreated out of the room.

Hanna gave the rope in her teeth one last tug and then jerked her hand through the opening she made with a wince. She scrambled over to him and started working on his own bindings, getting him free in a couple of minutes.

"When she comes in, we'll fight," Jori said, resignation heavy in his veins. "They're not going to take me as a hostage." *Not without you.*

He'd do anything if it meant that Hanna would make it, even submit to whatever tortures awaited him on Kilrym. But that wasn't what Zilly's father planned.

Hanna grabbed his face and kissed him fiercely, her warmth and ferocity pouring into him like energy itself. He let the kiss imprint on him, surrendering to it completely. His arms came around to hold her close, heedless of his injuries. Hanna was in his arms, he couldn't care about pain.

If they weren't tied up in a closet and facing imminent demise, he would have begged for more. Even with the threat hanging over them, he couldn't make himself pull back for some time.

After one breath or a hundred, it was Hanna who did. She smiled at him and let her forehead rest against his own. "I love you."

Elation warred with sorrow. *Yes, finally.* But there was no time to enjoy it, no time to celebrate this thing between them and what it could be. He'd known his job might ruin things for them, but he'd never imagined the ruination would come so soon.

He kissed her again, saying the words back between every breath.

Then she said three words neither of them had dared to broach. "Bond with me."

Their gazes locked. Hanna was utterly serious, and Jori's expression must have matched.

"We can't take that back," he forced himself to say.

Hanna shrugged. "Do you see another choice?"

He couldn't let that stand. "It would still be you, even if we weren't under this threat. I've been trying to think of a way to convince you for days."

She nodded. "Do it, Jori."

22

Hanna grasped Jori's hand. It wasn't strictly necessary and time was of the essence, but she needed the connection. A person wasn't supposed to undertake a Match in the heat of the moment, but she didn't see other options.

And she wanted this.

Wanted him.

If they survived past the next hour, they could figure out their future. Somehow. The imminent threat of death had a way of changing her perspective. What had seemed impossible only a few hours ago was now something she couldn't resist.

Jori's skin was warm against hers, his grip tight.

She wasn't exactly sure how the bond was

supposed to feel. It wasn't something that got talked about a ton. Back home, Matched units completed their bonding in privacy and rarely spoke of it. But that didn't mean there weren't rumors. And she knew the basics.

There he was.

She could feel Jori's power inside of her and gasped as her spark seemed to light her up from the inside. The hand that gripped her danced with lightning. Her spark, from his fingers.

Hanna let her eyes drift closed and sank into her center. She followed it deep inside herself until she found the place where she and Jori's power was bound together. There was a sort of protective shield keeping it blocked off. Jori had reached through from his side and taken some of her spark.

Now she reached through and grabbed for his.

The shield fell away.

Power surged through Hanna, stronger than she'd ever felt before. Her wings flared out, twice their normal size, and an uncontrolled burst of spark shot out and blasted the wall.

The wall didn't budge.

Hanna surged forward and kissed Jori as their power combined and grew. She didn't know why, but a Matched pair was somehow stronger than the sum of the bonded Zulir, power combining and growing to something nearly unstoppable.

Zilly, her father, and whoever else wanted to fight them didn't stand a chance.

They stood, hands still clasped, and faced the door. It was no match for their power and blew off its hinges with a single blast.

Their makeshift cell was a closet off of the main cabin, but no one was inside. All the evidence of Zilly and Kark that Hanna had seen before Zilly knocked her out was gone.

If she and Jori had waited any longer to check out this lead, there wouldn't have been any clues left.

They took the Apsyn standing outside the cabin by surprise, and he went down before he could call out an alarm. Hanna and Jori both wore their wings proudly, the edges of them dancing together and power sparking in a celebration of their bond.

Something hit her in the back, glancing off her wings, but the force hard enough to make her stumble. Hanna turned, raining down power at the group of Apsyns daring to attack her. Two were fried in an instant, while the final one took off running.

She had to drop Jori's hand as they covered fire from both sides.

Before their bonding, they'd already be dead. Now this was as simple as breathing.

She counted six men down, but no sign of Zilly. One of the men could have been Zilly's father, but Hanna doubted it.

Engines fired, the boom of ignition drawing her attention away from the remaining Apsyn. Jori took him out.

Then they ran.

The ship was a small vessel, meant for quick transport hops between Kilrym and Aorsa. Hanna would bet all she was worth that it had falsified papers and no connection to Zilly or her family.

It was a completely unremarkable hunk of gray metal. Hanna had seen thousands of similar ships in her time, and she wouldn't have thought twice of it. But this ship was the one that wanted to carry Jori away as a hostage.

Hanna wasn't about to let that happen.

She sent a blast of her spark at the right engine, but it glanced off.

"*Braznon's bowels*! It's shielded." Who put up their shields before the cargo bay door was closed? Shields worked against energetic strikes, not people. A team of soldiers could stampede onto the ship and capture the crew, shields be damned.

Hanna bounced on her feet.

"Don't do it," Jori warned, one hand gently placed on her arm. "I've got the ID number. We can track it now."

"They'll scrub that the second they land. You and I both know Zilly and her family will get set right back up. Whatever they're planning, all we did was take out lackeys. We have to stop them now." Jori wasn't holding her in place. She could make the run herself, but she didn't want to do it alone.

"Ah, *punt*." Jori dropped his hand.

They ran.

The engines were firing in their pre-takeoff sequence. Hanna and Jori still had a few minutes before it would be ready to launch into orbit. And the second Hanna cleared the loading ramp, she searched for a power box.

She couldn't kill the engines without getting to the engine room, but that wasn't the only necessary system on the ship.

An unobtrusive white box hung on the wall that separated the cargo bay from the hall leading into the ship. Hanna flipped it open and smiled at the switches before sending her spark out of her fingertips and breathing in the acrid scent of burning metal and plastic.

"Life support system compromised. Beginning self-repair," announced the ship's system.

"Smart." Jori nodded in approval as they continued into the ship.

No life support, no launch. Not unless their target was suicidal.

She and Jori had to move slower now. There'd been six Apsyns on the ground. Zilly was definitely still unaccounted for, and her father was most likely near her. The ship was small, but only in spaceship terms. There were multiple rooms, narrow halls, and easy places to corner anyone unfamiliar with the design, no matter how powerful they were.

Hanna strained to hear anyone coming their way. All she could make out was the whining siren of the failed life support system.

They walked by what passed for the armory, a small closet right off the sleeping quarters. The hooks were empty except for one blaster that was blinking a light that indicated it was broken.

The sleeping quarters consisted of two rooms of bunks, one on either side of the hallway. Four bunks and seats in each, though in each of the rooms, only three of the seats appeared used.

The corridor led up a small ladder and into the

cockpit. Or, Hanna assumed that was where it led. The door was sealed off.

She gestured towards it, then towards herself, and used a wing to shield her side. She'd breach, Jori would cover, and then this mess would be done.

Jori jerked his head from side to side and moved to stand in front of her. She glared and shouldered her way in front of him more forcefully.

Now was not the time for manly heroics.

The look Jori gave her spoke volumes, but after a moment, he relented and stepped back. The whole exchange took only a handful of seconds, but Hanna worried it was too long.

She charged up the ladder and blasted the door open, keeping herself shielded and bracing for hits that never came.

Once she scrambled up, she saw why.

An older Apsyn man had his arm around Zilly's throat, a small blaster pointed right at her temple. Blasters weren't meant to be lethal, but aimed at the head at that range, anything might kill a person.

Jori was up the ladder right behind her and froze when he took in the scene.

"The two Synnr agents." Zilly's father smiled. "I'm so glad you could join us. My dear daughter has told me all about you. My name is Varin." He didn't offer a family name.

Zilly struggled against him, and he squeezed tighter.

"The life support system is fried and your men are dead, Varin." Hanna kept her eyes on him, refusing to offer Zilly so much as a sympathetic glance. "Surrender now and you'll survive."

The smile didn't slip from Varin's face. "The ship is repairing itself. Give it a few more minutes, and I can limp out of here."

Zilly made a sound of protest that Varin ignored.

Hanna looked for an opening, some way to incapacitate Varin without taking Zilly out. But she was a very effective shield and Hanna couldn't risk it.

Zilly had betrayed her. She was an Apsyn interloper. But Hanna had left enough bodies in her wake. She didn't need to add one more.

"This doesn't have to be a fight." Jori was obscured half a step behind her and Hanna didn't look his way.

"It doesn't," Varin agreed. "Walk away. Tell your superiors I got away while you were fighting my men. No one else has to die. No one gets locked in a cage. This idiotic war lasts another day."

A few months ago, Hanna might have taken the

out. She didn't owe the Synnrs anything, and the Apsyns could rot.

But Varin was hurting people. "What's the play?" she asked. "You provide weapons and Kark provided people?"

"Ah, ah." His blaster shifted, and Zilly's eyes got impossibly wider. "You don't get information. That's not the deal. We all walk away with our lives."

Not happening.

Hanna lashed out, her spark aiming for the pilot's console rather than Varin. Flickers of electricity went up in acrid smoke and devastating pops as her power flooded the system and took out the controls.

Zilly screamed, and then her voice cut off in sudden silence. Her body went limp and she clattered to the ground. Dead.

Varin stared at the blaster in his hand for a long second, the look of grief on his face so profound that Hanna hurt for him, despite all the terror and pain he'd caused.

Despite the fact he'd just murdered his own daughter.

His wings flared wide and he swung the blaster their way. "She bumped me. Made me hit the trigger. It was—" he cut himself off, face firming into resolve.

"It's over, Varin." Hanna needed this to end. "Put the blaster down and vanish your wings."

Varin's gaze turned to her, but he wasn't seeing her. There was a manic glint to him, and Hanna braced for the attack. "Computer, this is Captain Varin Osdet. Initiate self destruct sequence theta."

"Negative!" Jori tried to belay the command.

The computer ignored him. "Command acknowledged. Alert, Captain. Three life forms are aboard the ship."

Varin choked out a sob, and his eyes flashed to Zilly for only a moment. "Affirmative. Override safety protocols. Override cancelation prot—"

"Stop this, Varin." Jori sent a burst of his spark at the man, but Varin blocked it with his wings.

"Override cancelation protocol," Varin spat out. "Confirm command."

"Command confirmed," the computer announced. "Self destruct sequence theta initiated."

"I didn't mean to kill her," Varin said. His shoulders straightened. "And she wouldn't want me to surrender." He nodded, and Hanna realized what he was doing the second before his eyes flashed white as he turned his spark inward, killing himself.

"Self destruct in fifteen seconds."

"*Braznon's bowels*. Run!" Hanna grabbed Jori before

he could do something heroic like try to recover one of the bodies or search them for any useful information.

They sprinted through the ship, and now Hanna was thankful it was a tiny craft. They didn't have time to move cautiously, and she hoped no one had snuck on board and was waiting to ambush them. Then they'd all be dead.

A sliver of daylight came from the door in the distance just as Hanna heard the rumble of the engines starting to implode.

She kept a tight hold of Jori's hand as they ate up the rest of the distance and she prayed to any spirit listening that they'd make it. They were so close. She could smell the fresh air.

And fire.

Hanna dove off the ramp, wrapping her arms tight around Jori and enveloping him in her wings as he did the same for her, using their spark as a protective cocoon as Varin's ship went up in flames around them.

The air hurt to breathe, it was so hot. But they were alive.

The bad guys were dead, their plans in ruins, and she and Jori had made it.

She kissed Jori, the elation of victory overpowering everything else. And Jori kissed her right back with all the strength she knew he had.

She didn't know how long they lay there, wrapped up in each other and unrelentingly happy for survival. It might have just been the two of them in the entire world, until she heard someone clear her throat.

Solan stood outside the perimeter of the wreckage, his Match, Lena, by his side. He raised both of his eyebrows and grinned at them. "So would you call this mission a success?"

"How'd you find us?" asked Hanna.

Lena was the one to respond. "We tracked the bikes. Major Ozar has a team following right behind us."

Jori wrapped Hanna even tighter in his arms and grinned over at both of them. "Yes. The mission was definitely a success."

23

It still felt weird sitting in an office, her desk opposite Jori. Hanna wasn't sure it would ever feel anything *but* weird. But she could feel the pulse of his power securely inside of her, and every so often he'd glance up at her and smile.

Maybe weird was okay for now.

"Are you finished with your write up?" he asked the next time he glanced over.

Hanna made a face. At least when they were undercover they didn't have to fill out paperwork. "They give you one tiny promotion and suddenly it's all work, work, work," she teased.

"That's not what you said on our lunch break." He gave her a sexy grin.

Her cheeks might have heated a little, but Hanna shot him a brash look anyway. "Yeah, on our *break*. We both know there's a perfectly good closet right down the hall."

"You just like the risk of getting caught." But he was grinning.

And maybe she did, a little. She'd learned more about herself than she'd expected on the mission, but all that really mattered was the most important thing she'd gotten.

Jori's heart.

With Morn Kark's operation in shambles, they were tying up loose ends. A few of his men were unaccounted for, but there was no indication of another bomb threat. Other agents were diving into the mystery of Varin Osdet and his enterprise.

"Any word on the smuggled humans?" she asked. She'd visited Sarah twice since the end of the job, and every time the girl asked about the other victims.

Jori shook his head. "It's on Felyx's team right now. But they're trying to make sense of the mess Osdet left us. We..." he trailed off and looked past her shoulder, the smile slipping off his face.

Hanna turned and saw a young blonde human woman standing next to a tall Synnr warrior.

Luci.

And Ax.

Hanna tensed. A part of her wanted to sprint for that oh so convenient closet and hide until they disappeared. She'd done them the kind of wrong that couldn't be forgiven. Luci and Ax had nearly died because of Hanna. She didn't get to apologize and say all was well.

Luci met her gaze, recognition clear. She didn't smile. How could she? But she gave Hanna a single nod before looking away.

Not absolution. Never that.

Acknowledgement.

Maybe that was a start.

Solan and Lena joined Luci and Ax after a moment, and they all left together.

"Are you okay?" Jori asked quietly.

"I don't think I'm the one you should ask."

He reached across their desks and placed his hand on top of hers, eyes serious. "Of course I should. Luci and Ax are doing well. She's not going to... I don't actually know what you think she might do."

Hanna thought for several moments. "Uh... cry? Yell? Just generally rant at me?"

"Luci's tougher than that. Sneakier too. I'd watch out if she ever corners you in a back alley."

Hanna scowled. "I don't know why I put up with you."

He laced their fingers together. "You love me."

"Against my better judgement." But she lifted up their joined hands and kissed his.

"Ready to head home?" he asked.

That was another thing to get used to. No more cell. No more guards—unless you counted the look Jori got on his face when there was only one cookie left. Just the two of them.

Together.

"Yeah, I'm ready." Hanna smiled. As impossible as it might have seemed, she was exactly where she'd always belonged.

———

Thank you for reading Synnr's Ride!

GET A BONUS SHORT STORY FEATURING HANNA & JORI!

You can get a free short story featuring Hanna & Jori by joining my newsletter. You'll also be the first to know about great deals and new releases.

Here's what you should read next:

Check out a new alien world in Crux, the first book in the Dragon Brides series.

WHAT TO READ
NEXT: CRUX

Prince Crux is in a bind.

When the Dragon King commands Crux find a mate, his days of carefree bachelorhood are over. One trip to a psychic matchmaker and he's on the path to his destiny. But it all comes screeching to a halt when he meets a human woman who lights his inner fire and makes him yearn.

She's got a pair of roller skates and an attitude.

Courtney is supposed to be putting the shambles of her life back together. Getting abducted by aliens isn't part of the plan. Neither is getting rescued by a scorchingly hot dragon that makes her think of an impossible future. But they have no chance together if they can't first escape a planet full of monsters intent on their destruction.

JOIN THE CELESTIAL HEARTS CLUB

HEY THERE, wonderful reader! Are you ready to take our relationship to the next level?

By becoming a member of the Celestial Hearts Club, you'll get access to early looks at new books, exclusive content, and sneak peeks that will make your heart skip a beat.

Plus, you'll be directly contributing to the creation of more epic love stories and heart pounding space adventures.

Are you ready to hop on board and support the creation of more out-of-this-world romance?

Check it out!
https://katerudolph.net/celestialheartsclub

Werewolf. Bodyguard. Mate.
The origins of these shifters are shrouded in mystery, but they're determined to protect their mates from any harm that comes their way.
Also available in audio!
Hunting Season
On the Prowl
Stalking Magic
Hungry for the Wolf

————

Stealing the Alpha

The thief takes what she wants, but the alpha keeps what's his...
Join shifter thief Mel as she clashes with lion alpha Luke in an explosive trilogy of two opposites who can't keep away from one another.
Also available in audio!
The Alpha Heist
Entangled with the Thief
In the Alpha's Bed

————

Alien Mates: Planet Exile

Guerran is no place for pretty human women. But these alien heroes will protect their mates!
Also available in audio!

Exile's Hunter
Exile's Adored

———

Zulir Warrior Mates

Kidnapped humans. Alien Warriors. Electric wings.
The Zulir Warrior Mates series brings you human heroines and heroes abducted from Earth who find love – and wings! – with the alien warriors who rescue them.
Also available in audio!
Synnr's Saint
Synnr's Hope
Synnr's Spark
Synnr's Kiss

———

Mated to the Alien

Fated Mate Alien Romance

Detyens are doomed to die young if they don't find their fated mates.

Follow along as these mated pairs fight off aliens, corrupt dictators, prejudiced humans, pirates, and more! The books can be read or listened to in any order, though some characters show up in multiple stories.

Select books available in audio.

Pick a book and jump into the action today!

Ruwen

Tyral

Stoan

Cyborg

Krayter

Kayleb

Shayn

Braxtyn

Doryan

Dekon

———

Detyen Warriors

Detya was destroyed a hundred years ago. These doomed warriors are out to find justice... and their mates.

The Detyen Warriors series brings you kick butt heroines, alpha alien heroes, fated mates, and relationships strong enough to span the galaxy!

The entire series is also available in audio!

Soulless

Ruthless

Heartless

Faultless

Endless

Alien Holiday Romance

Christmas... in space????

These alien holiday romances look beyond Earth's winter holidays and ring in the season across the galaxy!

Select titles available in audio.

Snowed in with the Alien Beast

The Alien's Winter Gift

The Alien Reindeer's Wild Ride

Trapped with her Alien Mate

Alien Outlaws

Outlaws, schemes, and love... it's all there in the Alien Outlaws series...

Andie Munster is sick of life on Ixilta, the planet she got dumped on after being abducted from Earth six years ago. And when the mysterious and dangerous Xandr shows up looking for a way off the planet, she's half-prisoner, half-co-conspirator in a wild rush to escape.

Rogue Alien's Escape
Rogue Alien's Woman
Rogue Alien's Secret
Rogue Alien's Legacy

Find more by Kate Rudolph at www.katerudolph.net

ABOUT KATE RUDOLPH

Kate Rudolph is a paranormal and sci-fi romance writer who lives in Indiana. She loves writing about kick butt heroines and the steamy heroes who love them. She's been devouring romance novels since she was too young to be reading them and had to hide her books so no one would take them away. She couldn't imagine a better job in this world than writing romances and sharing them with her fellow readers.

If you enjoyed this story, please consider leaving a review.